I0665248

CONFLICTS
Inside Caring 5

Volume Five

Struggles in life continue, a homeless man who makes good, cholera on a wagon train, finding gold on a mountain tour, earthquake disaster, dream sequences and many more designed to take you away from the here and now. If you didn't see reflections of yourself or someone you know in the previous volume, here is Book 5. Find what resonates for you.

Are You?

Amazed – Flattered – Disturbed – Horrified

Richard O. Benton

Roben Press

Conflicts, Inside Caring 5
Copyright © 2021 by Richard O. Benton

Contact:
Email: richardbenton3@gmail.com
Website: www.richardObenton.com

ISBN 978-0-9822424-8-3

THIS BOOK IS PRINTED ON ACID FREE PAPER.
PRINTED IN THE UNITED STATES OF AMERICA

Acknowledgements

Thanks to George P. Stearns, who proofread this collection. Thanks also to Bob Bonato of Bonato Design and Gary Gustavson for their comments on behalf of these stories. Thanks also go to Joe Keeney for his InDesign work and to Dan Uitti, in whom I have for years relied to keep me on this side of the digital divide.

Richard O Benton

Table of Contents

Bridges

Home at last. I drive through my covered bridge and the problems my business brings each day melt away. The old bridge always brings to mind another bridge, one I *didn't* cross many years ago. It is a daily reminder of a time when Lady Luck crossed my path. It's something I revisit often.

I'm a country gentleman today. Kurt Muller is my name. You have no doubt heard of me. I run the charitable foundation that bears my name and recently received national recognition for its work.

The bridge's old boards clack loudly as my tires pass over them and I shudder as a familiar emotion courses through my body. It turns my mind back twenty years.

Horror and deprivation I suffered as a younger man led me to that other bridge. I had nothing to look forward to. I thought I couldn't get any lower but that night it happened. I had to face death.

Homeless! It happened to others, not to me. Except that it did. The business world untethered me; cast me out. And as soon as I could no longer pay my way, society cast me away as it would any worthless thing.

My insurance job, the one the big bosses promised when they hired me would become my career until I retired, downsized me. More automation, they said; good for the company. Bad for people, though.

Depression followed. I lived on my earnings, but they don't last forever. My bank account depleted; no call for my skills, no job in sight. I owed rent I couldn't pay. My landlord evicted me.

I entered a hand-to-mouth existence, adrift, not alone, but all alone. I collected bottles and cans for what money I could get. Learning to fit into homeless society required a paradigm shift in my thinking. To fit, I must *accept* society's edict that I had no value.

We homeless were downtrodden, looked down upon as the lowest of the low, mentally kicked to the gutter by every suit that passed, by every disparaging eye that looked upon us.

Desperate, I considered crime, but my fresh-faced Oklahoma background gave me values I couldn't shed. I gradually fit in and became part of the community. Eventually I signed in at a shelter, but I couldn't be there all the time. They encouraged us to find jobs. Funny!

One night I wandered aimlessly down a

street in Hartford's north end hoping I would tire enough to sleep through an entire night without a bad dream bringing me bolt upright; a man in a dark hoody stopped me on the sidewalk. He stuck a gun in my face. All I could see were the whites of his eyes. Suddenly I faced a real nightmare. My heart stopped.

"Gimme all you money!"

The man had a grating voice. It promised violence. Crack head? Didn't matter. Nobody to fool with. I handed him my wallet and the man strode away into the darkness.

He didn't get much. I knew what my wallet held; a five dollar bill, expired license I couldn't part with, miscellaneous personal notes tightly folded in various pockets of the wallet and a picture of my dead parents. I regretted that loss.

I pictured the man pulling out the five and stuffing it in a pocket, then tearing the wallet apart looking for more and finally tossing it into some scraggly bush he probably couldn't find again if he wanted. I bet he didn't even look at the picture. The license? I didn't live there anymore.

A dollar and thirty-five cents. The bastard didn't get that. As low as I could go, I kept thinking about the change in my pocket.

Suicide, all that's left.

I headed for the Buckley Bridge. As I passed an all-night gas station and convenience store, I noticed a big Lotto sign on the thoroughly papered window next to the door.

What the hell, I thought. I used one dollar from my change, got a Powerball ticket and tossed the rest into the little penny holder at the counter. I wouldn't need it. I turned to go.

"Hey, man," the clerk called as I got to the door, "Lotto's coming on. Wanna watch?"

I didn't say anything, but I came back to stare at the overhead TV. I checked my numbers, 14, 12, 3, 42, 37, Powerball number 7. My eyes went wide. I felt dizzy. I stuffed the ticket into my pocket. My eyes shifted. Holy Mackerel, I had the numbers; all of them.

Act normal!

I left the clerk still watching TV. I headed directly for the shelter. I looked in every dark patch, every alley, expecting…attack, I suppose.

I made it back. I didn't sleep at all that night. I knew I had to appear at the Lottery office in Newington to claim the prize. Tired and rumpled, yet energized, I borrowed ten dollars from Madge, the young lady who ran the shelter. I told her I had a job offer and she believed me. I got a bus to Newington and walked the rest of the way to the Lottery place. I arrived fifteen minutes after it opened for the day.

Not trusting myself to speak, I handed my ticket to an official. He looked at it, turned it over and saw my name and address written there, asked me to prove who I was. I told him about being mugged the night before and told him the truth that my address was a shelter. He took some history from me and checked me out on his computer. Satisfied I was me, He grinned wider than I've ever seen.

The rest, paperwork, a video they insisted I watch and some very good advice about protecting my "holdings." The lottery guy suggested the first thing I should do is to contact a financial advisor and did I know one?

"Would you recommend one?" I asked. He did.

I thought about the mugger. I should thank him. I'd never have bought that Lotto ticket otherwise. $5.00 and my parents' photo would have to suffice.

My memory scene morphed into Chuck Stoltz's office in the downtown.

"You won the lottery. What are you planning to do with all the money?"

I remember standing uncomfortably; engulfed by the knowledge, part of me hearing this financial advisor, part of me miles away. My hands trembled as his question resonated in my mind. From destitute to multi-multi-millionaire, all because I chanced to buy a Lotto ticket as my final act before...I didn't want to think about it.

Chuck's office had the usual appointments and he seemed competent. The Lotto people said he was honest and wouldn't take advantage.

"I lived in an apartment for years in that anthill section of Hartford. I want a house. I want space. I want to leave those memories behind."

"Plans for the future?" Chuck asked.

"Done a lot of thinking last night. I have more money now than I could have dreamed about. I'm yanking me up by the bootstraps. I have a business in mind. I won't share that yet, but I will say I plan to help the needy. I've lived that scene first hand. I have to set myself up, recreate me, if you will."

"Sounds good. Sit a few minutes and I'll go over your options." I sat.

Winning a lottery prize changed my life forever. I'd risen above the underbelly of the world, but still felt attached to it. I would use my wealth to create a foundation. It would serve to ease some of the worst abuses the *have nots* in America were forced to live with.

Every day I would think about me with my hand out asking for food, maybe for a dollar to get a sandwich, maybe "any spare change, man…," or in passing a store with a "Hiring," sign out front and being rejected because my old, dirty clothes and unkempt beard turned them off.

Deprivation is an ugly word, and it spelled me. That's why I would never forget. Yes, I would make it my mission to help those who can't help themselves.

The memory I keep so close fades. I clear the

last plank on my covered bridge, park and walk to my door. Before I enter, I turn and nod to my bridge, my symbol of rescue from meaningless death, a new start and of the solemn mission it gave me.

I returned to the shelter and handed the young woman ten dollars with my profuse thanks. We stayed in touch.

My reminiscence done, I go inside and close the door. My wife calls from the kitchen. "Supper in five."

"Coming, Madge."

Wagon Train

The wagon train made slow progress into the new State of Colorado after a long, dusty trek through Kansas. Situated four wagons from the very end, a worried Calvin Dutts conversed with his wife. They agreed. He passed her the reins and mounted their spare mule and went to the front in search of the Wagon-master.

"Ho there, Mr. Walton. Could I have a word?"

"What's that, Calvin?" The big man turned in his saddle and smiled at the smaller man, but the smile left his face when he got a good look at Calvin's worried countenance.

"Mr. Walton, I think we should talk private." Walton barely caught the whispered return. Walton nodded and turned aside. They rode until they were out of earshot.

"What's going on, Cal?"

"My youngest, Jack's took sick. I'm thinking it might be the Cholera."

Walton stared at the man, his face giving nothing of the turmoil those dreaded words did to his insides.

"We'll go have a look." He turned to the very front and called, "Stop the wagons!"

The long procession came to a halt. People jumped down to stretch and check out their posses-sions or some squeak or squeal that promised trou-ble down the trail. Bear grease might be in order. The ground over which they traveled challenged the strongest construction.

The two guided their animals back down the line at an even pace; giving the impression that Cal's wagon had a loose wheel or a headstrong mule. Hap-pened often enough.

They passed two and four mule teams whose owners barely looked up from their hot, boring, never-ending job of staying in line and keeping the right distance. At this break parents tended their kids. All were lost in thoughts of their own. If they needed to hear something, they would, in time.

Several mothers shooed small children into the nearby scrub. The women watched their little boys unbutton and relieve themselves, glad for the diversion. Little girls went on the opposite side of the train to squat, but none got beyond the eyes of their protectors.

Dust and toil and close quarters shortened their young ones' childhoods. The dangers of the open hills and plains and the need to survive grew them up quick. No time for frivolity. Mind your parents. Watch where you step. Snakebite kills. Storms kill. An unwary moment kills. Such were the times.

Voted as the 38th State of the Union four years before by a bunch of starch-collared, dark suited gentlemen over at the Congress in Washington during President Grant's last year in office, the Santa Fe Trail they traveled remained dirt and ruts, well-marked only by the many that had passed before.

The two men arrived and found Calvin's wife absently holding the reins in one hand while she turned and mildly scolded her children, her face pinched with worry. Their two unthinking mules stood quietly in harness, awaiting instructions.

Walton called to her just loud enough to be heard. "Mrs. Dutts, Calvin said you got a sick boy in the wagon."

"He's mighty sick, Mr. Walton, burnin' up. I can't get any water down him."

"Let me get up there." The Wagon-master mounted the step and sniffed the air at the cover opening, got a sour vomit smell and then looked into the dim opening. Jack lay restlessly at the back of the wagon, his eyes closed. Even in the light that entered through the cloth above the high-board sides, he could see the boy seemed pallid.

Calvin's two other children sat near the front on coarse weave blankets. Evidently their mother decided to separate them at the first hint of trouble. *Good for her*, he thought. They sat and stared at the big man, who gave them a wink and then got down to business.

Speaking to the wife, he asked, "When did this come on?"

"During the night, not long from daylight. I put another blanket on him and he slept for a time, but threw up an hour or so later and then he had the squirts until he dried out. Then his fever came up."

Walton considered. He knew Cholera and this fit the symptoms he knew. Probably bad water. He focused on it.

Addressing Calvin, he said, "Where did you fill your barrel last?"

"Back at that muddy spring, couple days ago."

"Now where exactly at the spring did you fill it?"

"We were crowded out at the clear part, but we got a good take a few yards down from it. Figured I'd let the cloudiness settle over a couple of days and dip from the top and it'd be okay."

"Likely right, Cal, but you can't tell what animal's been soilin' the water and you shoulda waited until you could get in there for the better water."

"I know, but we got the order to move and I didn't want to hold up the train."

"You and your boys are okay?" He looked at the woman. She nodded. "Stomach rumbles, but we're good."

Walton considered. The two boys in front and Calvin and his wife seemed okay. He hadn't lost anybody yet and as Wagon-master he had to make the decision. He noted Calvin's youngest was a bit on the frail side.

"There's no doctor on this train, worse luck, but I'm thinking you got bad water. Better get rid of it when we circle for the night. I'll see you get a share from the others. Get Ephron behind you to give you a few cups of his right now. You got to get water in the boy. Mix it with a small hand of salt. Won't taste good but that should help. I see you're keeping your other kids away and that's a good thing. Put your belongings to sun and air whenever we stop and ride it out. Next river we come to, about three days, get everything out and scrub it good. "

"How long, you think, Mr. Walton? This is my boy, you know."

"Likely a week, Calvin. If you can keep it contained to your wagon, I won't have to separate you from the train. You heard the instructions when we set out, didn't you?"

"Yes, I heard them. Out here it's likely my family's death isn't it?"

"Cholera is contagious. You'll have to be real careful to keep your Jack isolated. I don't want you gone any more than you do, Calvin. I'm responsible for the entire wagon train. If it spreads beyond your wagon, I'll have made a bad choice. You have to make sure it doesn't."

An uncomfortable silence lengthened between them. Finally, Calvin looked down and said, "I'll do as you say." Walton heard defeat in every syllable.

"Tonight I'll have to tell the camp that we have a sick, cramped up boy in your wagon and to stay away for the time being just to be safe. I'll tell them you have things in hand and that'll be a relief to the rest. You'd panic knowing some other wagon had sickness, so you'd feel the same way they would hearing of yours, wouldn't you?"

"Of course, Mr. Walton. Thank you, Mr. Walton," Calvin said.

"Just take care of the boy. Get that water. It'll come out all right." The Wagon-master nodded to Calvin and tipped his hat to Mrs. Dutts, turned and shouted up the line, "Get 'em moving." He rode away.

Whips cracked over the tops of the animals, and with creaks and groans the wagon train got underway again, unsmiling, dusty men at the reins and half the day's run yet to go.

A Hand Up

Light filtering through denuded oaks and ash trees create a dark confusion that makes the trail hard to see. As I shush along on my cross-country skis I take note of the tall, snow-laden pines standing still in the morning hush. Ahead I see a black mound in the snow right in the middle of the trail. I don't recall seeing it before. It's out of place. It reminds me of…

Let me back up. It's my first outing alone since my knee healed. I kiss my wife goodbye; toss my skis and poles into my trusty Subaru and drive into the 4000 acres of protected forest, lakes and meadows of Whites Woods, only minutes from my home. The roads are snow-covered, but no problem. I'm filled with anticipation. My replacement knee feels great. I feel great. I breathe in lungfuls of crisp forest air.

I park in one of the convenient places the Conservation Center has cleared near a trail I love. I reflect on the history of the place. Many years before, Alain and May White donated several thousand acres to the local populace to be held in perpetuity for lovers of nature. Those of us who know their story send a silent, "Thank you" to them every time we walk through the nature preserve they have saved for us.

I'd been off my skis since last season. Yesterday's snowstorm didn't dump big wet flakes or icy pellets; no, it deposited a half foot of perfect skiing snow. The day after the storm arrived clear, bright, cold and bracing. In other words, ideal. I have on my new NorthFace jacket, insulated leggings that bulk me up, my favorite Thinsulate, self-heating gloves, and, of course, my sunglasses to avoid snow blindness. I feel strong. The cold air buoys me up.

Now this…anomaly!

There are bears and beavers and coyotes and yes indeed, mountain lions in these woods. I know this. The others avoid humans like we smell bad. Maybe to them we do. They're not a bother, but bears like honey and birdseed left in plastic feeders and they love trash people don't put away properly. They have become used to people living in or near their habitat. Nonetheless, bears should be sleeping at this point.

I'm pushing forward on level ground. I'm cutting new snow on my Rossignol cross-country skis. Only the metronomic swish of the skis under my feet breaks the silence of this serene winter scene.

I see the mound fifty feet from me. I stop short. I squint through my sunglasses and lean forward a few inches. A couple pounds of snow in the fir tree above me takes that moment to drop down my neck.

"Yow…!"

I yell and paw at the stuff as it starts to melt. I look up again. The mound stands up and slowly turns a half circle to face the inadvertent noise I made. It stares at me. It's bigger than huge. It's the biggest black bear I've ever seen!

Robert Frost's famous poem, Stopping by Woods on a Snowy Evening absurdly runs through my mind. "The woods are lovely, dark and deep…"

A shiver wracks my frame. I'm no match for a cranky bear. That's where the poem breaks down. I don't have miles to go before I sleep and the only promises I gave my wife before I left were that I'd take my cell phone and be careful not to fall.

I'm on skis. I couldn't outrun a bear in racing shorts, but I better get ready to beat feet. I'm in six inches of new snow. I'm wearing ski boots. They are not sneakers. You either stand in them, walk awkwardly a few feet to the Ski Lodge's bar to bring back drinks for you and the cutie who said yes when you asked if she'd like to have a drink with you, or you could snap them in place on skis like their designed for. Okay, she's my wife now, all right?

What do I do if the bear charges me? I could remove my skis and whack him with one. That's one idea. If it didn't discourage him, I might survive a bit of pawing. Three-inch claws? I don't like that idea.

I could huff and puff and try to scare the creature. Yeah, Dick, huff and puff, why don't you? I could stare him down but I'm already convinced he stares better. No option seems quite right for this situation.

Oh, oh. The bear starts for me. I'm not a coward, but I'm thinking I should get in training to become one. I gulp.

Wait, something's wrong with the picture. The bear lumbers towards me on all fours, not fast, and his gait is strange. What's happening here? The big old thing seems to be in pain. I don't connect at first, and then I get it. I begin to see red dots in the snow on the bear's right side. He's injured.

My whole attitude changes. I hope my adrenalin response disappears before he gets in range. Animals hate the smell of fear and I know fear pumps adrenalin into the tissues and that is what they smell and it does something to them, kicks in the fight or defend response which usually sends them into a rage. I saw a dog do that once. It's scary.

I can't believe it. Mr. Bear approaches me, sits on his haunches and extends his right paw. Holy crap, he wants me to help him. Shazam! I turn into Captain Marvel. No, I have to be dreaming, except I'm not willing to believe that I dreamed of coming to Whites Woods in the first place. It's too real not to be true. Better play along.

I examine the bear's paw and there's a sharp wood chip embedded between the first and second digits of its pad. It's bleeding a lot. I never did this before but I know what I have to do. I take the paw in my hand. I marvel at the length of that claw, but I look into the bear's eyes and I see acceptance of me, of its predicament, of the unusual connection he is requesting of a human and a woods creature like him.

It needs pliers. It's very deep. I don't carry pliers in my ski outfit, silly me, but given time I have enough to grasp that I could work the piece out of the tender area and remove it. I look into the bear's eyes again and feel his permission.

"It's going to hurt," I say conversationally.

The bear nods. Wait a minute. Bears don't nod. Yeah, well this one did. I go to work. It hurts a lot. My new friend grunts and pulls back from pain, but then returns his paw to me. My hand is bloody and it gets slippery. I lose track of time. Finally I feel the embedded part begin to move and I work it out. Success! I am exhausted. The bear is too.

I've done my thing and boy do I have a story to tell. The bear sits back and licks the blood away. After a bit he puts his paw in the snow, gathers and pulls himself up.

"So why were you out of your lair," I say, kind of smart-ass like.

"It was a lovely morning for a stroll is all I can say," the bear returns. He puts a paw across to shake my hand.

It turns into my wife's hand. She's got hold of mine and she's pumping it up and down.

"Dick, are you ever going to get up?"

No Easy Way Out

The snow felt great as my Arctic Cat plowed the deep, well settled mountain pack. Here I could make speed through widely separated pine trees. The dual tracks bit into the snow like teeth and devoured it, spitting it behind me. I thought of all that power under me, my sweet s'mobile plying woods and fields and mountain terrain and it brought a happy smile to my lips.

I topped a rise and stopped. Two choices: a long flat stretch or a downhill with a neat upturn. The hill looked smooth beyond it. I picked the second option. Not the best choice. That "neat upturn" fooled me with a five-foot drop-off. At forty-five all I could do was to yell, "Yahoo!" and put my weight back to balance my landing.

I stopped with no problem, but realized instantly I couldn't get back the way I'd come. From this angle, the ridge went in both directions as far as I could see.

How did I get in this fix?

Two reasons come to mind. First, I hit the jump. It dropped me into a long, snow-filled crevasse. I had to find another way out. I'm not going to comment on how stupid I was to assume beyond where I could see.

Well, hell, I'm here, might as well... I searched down and down looking for an easy way back, but the gorge twisted and rose, dropped, narrowed and enticed me. Before I stopped and got smart, it had led me far astray. By the time I got to a good turnaround, I was miles below my entry point. My watch said a few minutes before noon, not much, but I had hours of daylight left, so what the hell, I kept going, loving all that rugged beauty.

I finally began to worry and maybe get a little sense. I was in mighty big country without a clue how to get out. My terrain map didn't help. The mountains looked pretty much the same, a mosaic of white and craggy dark. I'd made many twists and turns and taken one fork or another, wily-nilly. The sun being on top of the sky didn't help and I couldn't be certain of compass directions because of iron in the surrounding mountains.

An old sourdough I'd met a couple of years before had entertained me with his stories. He said a good eye was better than a compass because of the iron.

I looked for features, odd-looking black patches on an otherwise white world, the kind I could remember. Dotted throughout I avoided the heavily drooping, snow covered green of the mountain forests. In the last hour I'd called myself an idiot six ways from Sunday for going off by myself with a ten-gallon gas can strapped to the back, outfitted with cold weather gear and no tent.

My bright red down jacket, yellow helmet and black backpack contrasted sharply with the terrain, but what good would that do? Maybe a hunter wouldn't shoot me? Besides, there weren't any hunters so far out and if there were, they were lost, too. Colorado is a big state and its share of Dinosaur National Monument with Utah didn't look big on a map, but believe it, it's big.

I thought back to my mid-morning conversation with my older brother Jed. We'd done a short morning run and I'd told him that I itched to make one more run for the day. He said the weather forecast for later included a deep freeze and a stiff wind. He told me the wind chill would be brutal and he wasn't going to chance it.

"I'll be back in four hours," I said.

"Don't do it, Jake. You're not experienced enough."

"C'mon, Jed. I can handle it." I waved him off, fired up my rig and tracked away without looking back. He'd forgive me later. Jed had a soft heart.

I mentioned two reasons. The other one? The wind. It picked up right on schedule, but I didn't realize it would cover my tracks so completely. I bit my lip as I thought of Mom and Dad. They were in

Europe for a couple of months with Dad on business. He took Mom along on holiday. They knew we were going into big country to a lodge we'd all been to before and they trusted Jed to be my brake. Didn't work.

I'm eighteen and Jed's six years older and a lot more experienced, even I had to admit. Yeah, I should have listened to him. He knew how impulsive I could be. Eighteen is only a number, but it grew pretty big as I began to realize eighteen wasn't grown up, not grown up at all. Bit of a shock to the system being honest with myself.

My clothing kept me warm so long as I was on the move and using energy, but I could feel the temperature going down. Jed had said it would be all minus numbers by the time I got back and don't mess with the wind chill, either. He meant helmet and gloves better stay attached to the rest of the outfit.

All my thoughts didn't help. I got more nervous as I realized nothing looked familiar. It wasn't a big mental leap to figure out that perspectives changed all the time, so I couldn't rely on features as a clue to my way out.

Up ahead the pass opened out and got flat. Had to be a lake, yeah, there!

I stopped, got out my terrain map again and tried to place the new feature. The gloves were clumsy and the wind had picked up a notch, making it hard to hold, but I didn't dare take them off. My hands were already cold and frostbite ain't fun.

I hunched down near the side of my Cat and spread it out on the snow. The wind tore at the edges, but in a couple of minutes, I'd traced out the lodge and made some guesses about my compass direction.

"Right there, Jake."

I put a gloved finger on the spot and my heart sank. I had to be…that far away? I didn't believe it, but no other feature looked like it. I'd run stupid for thirty miles? What fun; I could die. Big country kept on going and my map showed no settlements or mines or ranger stations for way too many miles.

"You were right, Jed," I breathed.

It became important to hear myself. I didn't want to admit it, but the truth lay in front of me now. I reached into a side pocket and took out my last energy bar. I'd have to munch slowly, maybe even save some for later.

This was serious. Think, Jake. You got yourself into this, now get out. You're not as bright, but you're strong and you've got a brother waiting, and a Mom and Dad who aren't expecting to read about you in the newspapers.

Slow fear crept toward my heart and I shivered.

No, Jake, can't do this! You want to tell this story to your grandchildren, right? If you can get here, you can get back.

I plotted a course, watching the terrain altitude markers closely. No more lark. Now it's survival.

I checked my watch. Three hours out. Take another three, minimum. Might run out of gas. Better conserve, starting now. Let's see, I left at ten-thirty. It's one-thirty. Three hours would put me into twilight. I had to be about two miles out when I jumped that ridge. If I could make it back there, I might have to leave the Cat and hoof it, but two is better than thirty.

Yeah, another thing. At four hours, Jed would be really antsy. By five, he'd have a search party out looking. He saw me take off and I'd bet a dollar he watched me until I disappeared. Somewhere in there he would have waved his hands in disgust, like, I'm washing you off, kill yourself, freeze to death, I don't care.

But he did care and he wouldn't do that. I loved my brother and he loved me. He'd be pissed and go into the lodge and have a cool one or three and probably make talk with ladies we always found at upcountry lodges not brave enough to rough it, but hopelessly in love with rugged terrain and mountain spawned daredevils.

They knew what they wanted and we did, too, so like cats they waited in warmth by the big hearth fire. We'd arrive exhilarated from our long runs on our purring Cats and spend an evening with a different kind.

Jed…the Rangers…they'd be looking for me. Jake, old man, all you have to do is to hold up your end.

I took a deep breath, spun my Cat around and headed back the way I came.

Thoughts around a Batch of Brownies

The Brownies tasted different this time. Lizzie had made one batch before this one today, but this time something was missing. They didn't taste right.

Maybe, she thought, *I didn't put in the exact measure the recipe called for but so what.*

She'd been making off the cuff meals for forty years and better and no recipe book's going to tell me how to make brownies. Hadn't she raised five children, and didn't they all go on to make successful lives?

Why, Mandy, the oldest, held a high-placed job in a big insurance company. She's in charge of some corporate something-or-other department with a lot of people under her, even men. Not like it used to be with men telling us women how to get along and what to do. Big responsible job. Yep!

'Course, she's in California now and I haven't seen her in two years.

Last time she called - I think four months ago - she said she was too busy to write. Too busy to call either seems like. That's a downside.

They shouldn't be working her like that.

Lizzie set the tray of brownies on the broad windowsill to cool and glanced over her familiar scene, a low hill with row upon row of tall, healthy corn on the right and rows of beets, lettuce and radishes on the left. Couldn't figure it, but radishes were big in the market this year. Not up to her to guess the market. Her boy would do that.

Her gaze lingered on the hill yonder. Alvin, her youngest, up there plowing the fallow field under for next year's crop. She could just see the red polka-dot bandanna he always wore atop his head over the corn tassels as he sat in the bucket seat of his dad's old Farmall tractor wielding that big, flat wheel.

She watched him flick it off his head, its polka dots making an odd pattern against the blue sky. She loved the way it circled his head before he gathered it to wipe his sweat. It reminded Lizzie of Zack cracking the old whip and yelling, "Gee" and "Haw!" to the horses. No plow horses anymore. There, Alvin wiped his brow, flicked it again and stuffed it into his shirt pocket. Just like Zack.

The brownie she ate made a little lump somewhere inside. She could feel it and it didn't set right, went down bitter. She walked over to the stove to make sure she'd turned it off. She forgot now and again. The big kitchen didn't have much modern stuff in it; a blender that sat on the far edge of the chopping block and the electric stove that replaced the old wood stove, and of course the new iron Alvin, the practical sort, gave her last Christmas.

My, how good it worked. Still, the rest of the kitchen hadn't gotten out of the nineteenth century and so far as she cared, the kitchen fit her and she fit the kitchen. She thought of the day the kids gave up trying to change things.

"Ma, be so much easier for you," they said.

"You don't worry none. I like what I got and what I got's good enough."

They finally understood their old Ma. It made her smile.

The 1740 brick farmhouse sat near the edge of Doneley Road, maintaining its fourteen room presence on a highly successful four hundred acre farm her cantankerous farmer husband Zachariah Doneley had wrested from the soil by his sweat and sometimes by his blood over forty hard years. He died twelve years ago; heart. Difficult, opinionated, but a good and God-fearing, Sunday church-going man.

She'd took up her time being busy with the house and the grandkids and never thought about spending some of the insurance money from that policy Herb bought in the forties after the big war to update anything. It's sitting in the bank drawing interest, and that's fine.

She didn't want to upgrade. What could be so awful about hand pumping that sweet well water? Why, the pump sat right next to the sink and it never froze during the winter. Wasn't like she had to make a trip down to the well like she did when she and Zack were first married, and it only took a cup of water to prime it. She kept a water-filled milk bottle with a paper cap setting next to it yonder.

My idea, she thought smugly.

Pumping, is it a trouble? No, no trouble at all.

She went back to her train of thought. Mark is in the Army. Always wanted to be in the military like his Pa, even though he'd not got into any wars to speak of yet. Zack had been proud of being a dog-foot, but Matt had bigger ideas and good for him.

First Lieutenant now and if he plays his cards right, he'll be Captain by next year. After that you keep dealing those cards in the right places and you start getting noticed. He's a bright boy. He'll make his way all right.

Chloe, my youngest is a dancer up in Chicago. She writes me once a week, no matter what. I haven't heard about that exotic dancing thing she told me she does, but it must be pretty important out there, because she told me what she makes and it's a lot!

Bobbie, now that one may be president some-day. He's always trying out his political theories on me when he and Claudette come to visit with the three grandkids, and his ideas are so interesting and sound so right. He works at a polling place right now between jobs, but he's a staunch Republican and last time we spoke he said to me that the committee is looking at him and maybe he'll be a candidate in the local election come November. My, my, how about that! My handsome Bobbie. Bet Claudette's glad she got hold of that one.

She scrubbed at the pans and tins with a will in the old soapstone sink and soon enough they looked shiny again. Dutifully she plucked a brownie from the now cool tray and munched it. Not bad; the bitter aftertaste was less pronounced than when it was hot. How to get rid of that? Sugar, of course. She glanced at the recipe book, still open to the correct page.

Cat distracted me jumping up on the counter and had to put her off. Maybe I forgot the sugar. Can't be absent-minded. Next batch I will watch the sugar. Out this one goes.

Decided, she pulled the full tin off the sill and dumped it into the trash. She glanced at the clock. Near twelve. Alvin would be quitting in a few minutes with the sun overhead. Better get at making him his lunch. She hummed a few bars of, "When the Roll is Called Up Yonder...," as she grabbed ingredients she knew he'd like.

Such a comfort, knowing at the end she'd be going to her God. She'd cut Alvin a big piece of brownie out of the new tin soon's it's baked and put it into a plastic bag for a snack later on the hill. He'd like that, yes he would. And speak of the Devil, here he comes.

She watched her lanky twenty-seven year old

in bib-overalls saunter down along the dirt path from the hill and when he saw her in the kitchen window he smiled and waved. Zack taught him a lot and he's taken the reins in his hands and he's doing just fine. What a fine boy.

Lizzie set a small table for her and Alvin in the kitchen. He stomped in, shucked his boots and went to the sink where he took considerable time washing his hands. He came back and sat in his chair.

"Looks good, Ma."

The smell of him, sweat and grass and that wonderful, rich earth on his overalls wafted across her nostrils.

Love all my kids, she thought, but how lucky I am to have my Alvin here with me. Life is good.

The Nugget

On May 9th, while walking with a group of thirty congenial strangers on a guided tour by Mid-Western out of Albuquerque I got separated.

"Got" isn't right; I wanted to. I get bored – seemed like I'd seen that, done that – so I looked around for a little diversion. We had on tall, leather hiking boots under dark pants and white short-sleeved shirts, evidently the day's dress of choice for hot country infested with rattlers.

The tour company provided them as protection. The occasional rattler might scare our heavy-footed city-slicker crowd into behaving badly. Our guide, a loose- limbed cowboy named Matt, said we wouldn't likely see any, but he carried a long barrel forty-five at his hip and matter-of-factly mentioned before we set out that you had to be prepared for anything in the hills.

"I'm an expert shot, folks. Don't worry," he said.

The ghastly little camouflage print backpacks they provided along with the boots and our outfits made me think of parochial school children on a field trip. The rest of the outfit we brought, cameras and compasses and other pocket junk, and our group flashed "Tourist! Tourist! Tourist!" like a neon sign.

I carried an outsized bag with my new digital camera and other stuff I really didn't need to bring along. "Better safe than sorry," my motto.

The fainter of heart looked around furtively as if to say, "How do I get out of here?" but no one bolted and Matt had such a ho-hum attitude about "them varmints" as he called them, that the group settled down quickly. We also carried rain slickers under our packs, yellow; light plastic and easy to see. They didn't take up much room, but got a few grumbles anyway.

Matt told us that we were in the rainy season. Everyone looked around and smiled. It couldn't have looked drier if we'd been in Death Valley. I was just happy the rain gear wasn't the old, smelly, heavy, oil-soaked canvass kind.

"Afternoon storms blow up quick this time of year," he told us. "Keep y'all from a ten-second soaking when they come."

One of the younger members of the tour – I forget who – said, "Ten seconds is nothing!"

Matt turned to him. "It is out here, chappy." You could tell that statements made by people who didn't know what they were talking about irritated him, but he probably figured, you get who you get on a tour, so he raised his voice to the crowd, "Any questions before we light out?"

Everyone wanted to be on the way, so nobody said anything.

"Let's go!"

Matt turned and walked to the trailhead. A weathered old sign said Devil's Fork Trail and pointed the way. Matt had nothing more to say to the tightly packed crowd. As we walked single file through the narrow, rocky entranceway, husbands and wives or friends spoke in low tones, glancing one way and then another, smiling and pointing while taking in the breathtaking scenery.

Occasionally Matt answered a question somebody called out. He let the scenery do the rest. I got the impression Matt wasn't much on talking and I wondered how he'd come by a job as a tour guide, but he sure knew his mountains!

A couple of hours into the six-hour hike we stopped for lunch. Everyone dutifully took out their pre-packaged sandwiches and unwrapped them. I forgot to mention we had been fitted with canteens. Some of the group wanted sodas, a couple or three wanted to take beer or a bottle of wine along, but Matt wouldn't bend the rules.

"Out in the wilderness," he told them, "water is the staff of life."

Our prepackaged meal, courtesy of Mid-Western Tours – what else – also contained something like the beef jerky us city dwellers could find in any Seven-Eleven, but which was much more important here. There it was saturated fats and big bellies. Here nourishment preserved life.

The meal satisfied most of us and I ignored the usual complainers. They just didn't get it.

We packed our debris at the order of our guide. Matt wouldn't let even one little wrapper stay to imply that anyone had been there. By now, everyone realized Matt could very well leave us and we'd be in a world of hurt trying to find our way back to civilization. More with silence than with words, he grabbed our fear of the unknown with a fist and held every one of us tight. His mercy, although he probably thought "pity," would return us to our cars so we could leave this land of beauty and raw, sometimes deadly nature.

The gorgeous hills and valleys, with their subtle and variegated golden colors proceeded down, down, down into a cleft that seemed to narrow with each step, and the view darkened subtly. I heard murmuring; some of us had become uneasy again.

For me, I became more excited, because an idea began to form in my mind and I loved it. I would slip away from the crowd and explore on my own. Just a little. Then I'd run back to the group and join again. Who would know the difference? Gradually, appearing interested in a rock formation or some other design of nature so as not to draw attention, the pack moved ahead of me.

Watching the looming formations closely, I saw a slit in the rock face. Above it, I could see light. It went somewhere. I glanced at the group. They moved steadily ahead. Quickly I stuffed myself into the slit. With barely enough room to move, I forced parts of me to fit its general contours and disappeared completely. It narrowed more above me and then widened out. Many years of accumulating dust had filled it enough to create a comfortable walkway.

I strolled along. It didn't appear used. I had taken a chance. The guide knew how many people he had, but with the winding character of the gorge, I figured he'd have to wait until they found a wide place to regroup before he would do a headcount again, so I had minutes at least.

Now on my own, I looked carefully into shadows and above at small platforms in the rock, watching for rattlers and scorpions. The rocks were dead, but I felt alive!

Less than a minute into the cleft, my eye caught a glint of something a little above eye level and I went over to inspect it. The object sat in a hollow. Generally round with more or less smooth pits in it, it beckoned me to touch it. I checked the fissure for anything else I didn't want to touch and then picked it up. I hefted it and figured it around ten pounds, heavy for its size. It seemed like a slightly different rock at first, but I got out the little Boy Scout knife I always carry and scratched it a little. Holy smokes!

Yellow, like gold! Could it be? I stood stock-still in denial.

Couldn't be!

I made a quick decision. I pulled the excess junk out of my camera case and the lump fitted nicely into the empty carrier. I hated to discard my stuff and I hate even more to litter, but I had to catch up and I knew it wouldn't be a good idea to let on about what I'd found. Besides, I also knew about iron pyrite, and I didn't want to be a laughing stock here or at home. No, I'd keep it to myself.

I made my way back to the point where I'd left the group. The ten-pound object pulled heavily at my shoulder strap, but my elation overcame whatever discomfort I felt.

Turning right, I trotted after my party. I found them milling around in a rift area. Matt had evidently stopped and taken a headcount and found me missing. He had just started back when I appeared.

"Where you been off to, soldier?" he asked.

"Had to relieve myself. Sorry."

"No problem, but stay close. Y'all can get lost out here in big country."

"I know. I'm sorry."

My lie seemed to do it for him and he returned to the front of the group. The others were intent on their own quests and didn't give me any more thought. Good. I didn't want to answer any questions. No one noticed that my camera now hung from the strap at my wrist or that my camera bag seemed full…and heavy.

I turned inward. Maybe I'd just come into my inheritance. My thought train deepened into how to deal with it. I could smelt the rock down and extract the gold and form an ingot. I knew how.

The market price of gold? The government owned this piece of real estate. Did that mean I had no right to my find? What if I walked into a government assayers office and they asked me where I'd found the big nugget? I hand it to them to look at and they say thank you. They look it over.

I reach for it back and I'm told, "Sorry, government property!"

My mind rebelled. The government already took too much of my money. It didn't think so but I did. I decided to be selfish and generous. The Gov wouldn't get any, but I would become secret benefactor to friends and relatives who needed money.

I'd put some away into a few accounts and then close them over time while investing in the stock market. I'd read about the bull market. People were doing well, of late. Now, how to sell it? People didn't hand a bank teller ten pounds of pure twenty-four karat gold and say, "Cash this for me, please."

I imagined a new course name at my college. How to Appear Suspicious 101. Hah!

What would I tell my wife? She'd stayed

behind with her mom and dad at the lodge. They were taking a last trip across the country with us. Dad's old knees didn't work well any more. Mom wouldn't leave him alone. I wanted Devils Fork Trail, they didn't and Lisa, only lukewarm to begin with, stayed behind. Plenty of entertainment at the lodge! I'd figure out what to tell her later.

We entered Devils Fork just beyond the gap. A mountainous, nearly vertical rock split the trail into three equal parts, reminiscent of a three-tined pitchfork and easy to see how the trail had gotten its name. Mountains climbed high all around us, and the entire group felt as daunted and diminished as I did.

Matt took a little time to explain who had found and named it and what significance it had in the preserve. He let us ramble around for a half hour looking at things and then called us together.

As we had finished out last descent, I looked up and noticed that a few clouds had appeared overhead. Ten minutes later, as we arrived at Devils Fork, I noted that the sky had dimmed and puffy clouds now covered the light blue sky from end to end.

I watched our leader for a couple of minutes. He looked up a couple of times. I noticed that Matt had lost a little of his aplomb. If I were guessing, I'd guess that he seemed worried. Unconvincingly, to me anyway, he addressed the group.

"Time to head back. Y'all feel ready?" he

smiled. "Rules are, you walk down, you walk back. I carry nobody; nobody carries me. Seems fair." He smiled again.

One, a slight and graying woman said, "Oh dear, do we have to climb much?"

"Only as high as you came down," Matt said. A few, mostly men, chuckled.

Then Matt offered a tiny encouragement. "Going up's not so hard. We'll set a spell if we need to, okay?"

The woman nodded and gulped. I'd never see her on a trail again.

On the way back, the nugget seemed to weigh more with each step. I casually changed shoulders from time to time and that relieved my fatigue. Matt noticed after I'd changed over for the fourth or fifth time.

"What you got there, gold?" he asked.

I replied quickly, "Camer...ah...yeah, gold. Want to carry it awhile?" My deliberate slip and the truth threw him off just as my lie had before.

No thanks," he said. "You brought it, you can bring it back."

Probably thought I was a smart-alec and he paid me no mind from then on. Good enough!

Then a flash of light and a crash of thunder!

Matt shouted as we began to hear again. "Put your slickers on now. Don't tarry!"

Tarry, quite a word for our semi-silent guide,

I thought. He was right, though. The sky opened up and buckets of rain poured on us, like from a faucet. I'd never seen so much rain come down all at once. The man knew the territory every which way.

Except for being genuinely tired when we got back to the lodge, my spirits couldn't have been brighter. My wife and her parents greeted the intrepid explorer brightly, too. Six hours on the sun deck and several glasses of wine saw to that. My wife asked me how it went and how I liked it.

"Great! Like finding ten pounds of pure gold," I said, and smiled mysteriously.

Family Affair

Dear Mom,

Mary here. Your daughter, remember? The picture of my family I've enclosed with this letter may shock you, as I never let on to anyone at home I had a family. Today is an anniversary of sorts. What is today? Keep reading; you'll find out.

I forgive you for all the pain you caused before I left Oklahoma twenty years ago. You just didn't understand me. Dad did, but he could never overcome your shallow-minded prejudices. He was a nice man, the husband you drove to the grave. You didn't think I knew that, did you? I've been getting reports from a good friend for years. Who? One never gives up a good source. Look around, make a few guesses. You won't find out.

Yes, I could only relate emotionally to girls. You thought of me as different. Other words you used on me in private and in public were weird or peculiar, but your favorite word as I recall was *queer*. Don't deny it. In those days people reacted to such differences by shaming them. Shame, oh yes, you did lots of that. Your narrow-minded upbringing forbade...never mind, I'm sure you know what I'm talking about. You never questioned, always went with the easiest route. You just went along, Mom.

When I heard you were in the hospital being treated for cancer I grabbed at it. My hatred for you welled up in me and for a time I became you, a callously cruel, vicious woman. I wished you ill. I descended into your dark world. I hoped you would live with unbearable pain until you were no more.

But I had Alma, my wife, my beloved, my rock. She recognized my symptoms and brought me out of it. Would that Dad could have straightened you out. We'd probably have had a wonderful life.

Let me introduce you to my family. Hold the picture in front of you. Look at us. Beside me is Alma. She is a fine example of dark Americana, having been raised in the New York City suburb of Queens by a dock worker and an exotic dancer who both abandoned her in early life to pursue their private interests and to hell with any incidental children they'd produced. Sound familiar, Mom?

Alma and I naturally gravitated toward one another when we met. We complimented each other. Together we healed each other. We, of course, never had children of our own, but we have both been successful in business and we both shared a desire for family.

As luck and government involvement would have it, we acquired three children through an adoption agency in Manhattan, each one a year apart, starting twelve years ago. It worked so well that we decided to become a focal point for more abandoned and abused children. Over the next few years we completed our family by adopting four very young children that we are raising with our sense of values. That's our limit, not that we couldn't have wanted more. We simply knew what we could afford.

The children are learning our brand of patience, caring, appreciation for others, compassion and integrity. They will form lasting friendships through right choices because we are showing them the way. They have tolerance, respect and commitment to family. Above all, they have love. It is what we shower them with daily.

How many of those can you claim, Mom?

Belinda, the oldest at 19, is in the center of the group. She's the one with the dark clothing and the sunglasses. She has a condition that requires that she wear darkened glasses all the time. I can't pronounce the name of her disease, but believe it, she can't take them off. She is not blind, but severely affected. She is at home and thanks to the Internet and her marvelous touch typing skills, she has a job she can work from the little office we made for her here and produces a good income. She is talented and sweet. We didn't throw her away because she was different.

The red-headed girl is our beloved Nancy. She has a job with an Ad agency in Manhattan and is doing a fantastic job. Her effervescent personality is a big plus. She ended up in State guardianship because her parents died in a boating accident and she had no relatives the State could contact. She's our daughter now.

Joan, at 17, has been a handful, but we understand her. Her crackhead mother OD'd and she never met her father. That's how she ended up in the system. Last week she told me she likes girls. I knew that, Mom, just as you did. I told her to go with how she feels. I told her that the conventions have changed and LGBTQ is out in the open around here. We are not going to shun her like you shunned me.

The rest of our girls, Amanda, Grace, Diane and Penny? From broken homes. The signs of abuse have all but disappeared because we have replaced their anguish with a comforting blanket of love. Love works, Mom. Love is the answer.

No point in your trying it now, I suppose, but maybe, like me, you could think about it and maybe you could soften your heart like I have. There may be some good left in your soul. Let's hope you find it before you get your final trumpet call.

I so wish you had been different. I wish you'd understood. I began to see my differences at thirteen. I had girlfriends. I rebuffed boys who tried to get to know me. They didn't repulse me. They simply didn't appeal to me. Today the psychology people tell us we are hardwired differently from what you called "normal" people. We can't help it, but that doesn't mean we aren't human. It doesn't mean we can't experience our lives and enjoy them and contribute.

Remember July 12, 1998, Mom, the day when at eighteen you screamed at me and hit me repeatedly with that big kitchen spoon and said all those vile things and how I left the house crying and didn't come back that night? I stayed with a friend. Remember that I came home the next day, went up to my room and packed a bag and left. You gave me silence and I gave it right back. My anger matched yours that day.

I walked up the street from our house. You didn't come out or call to me. That ended it. A girlfriend of mine, no, not a girlfriend like you're thinking, had parents who knew of your abuse. They picked me up at the corner and drove me downtown where I caught a Greyhound Bus for New York and I've been here ever since.

So why is today so important? It is because I left home twenty years ago today. I left you to your horrible thoughts, your mistaken facts and your un-forgiving nature and began to really live life.

I am sorry for you, as in pity, but I want to rise above such pettiness. I offer you a gift. My telephone number here in New York is 212-555-3365. If you want to make amends and you can bring yourself to it, call me.

Mary

The Strangest Dream

I floated somewhere between consciousness and sleep, the place of dreams. An empty wine glass glinted on the stand beside me. Farley's History of Steamboats lay on my chest as I slumped in my too-comfortable leather chair, interlaced fingers folded over the book, my page temporarily lost when I nodded off. The last passage I read started Chapter XI. The dream took over seamlessly.

I began to live the passage "The Silhouette stood out among a crowd of high-pressure steamboats clustered together on the Ohio River. Hills rose abruptly on either side of the river and from any high place; they looked like models floating in a bathtub."

I walked the gangway steeply, struggling with my suitcase, anxious and happy, an eighteen-year-old boy-man on his way to adventure. I graduated top of my class at Pittsburgh High School and I had all summer to decide on my college career: teacher or engineer. Tough choice, but I didn't have to make it until August.

To help, Mom and Dad decided to send me to

Aunt Gertrude's in Cincinnati to get me away from home pressures. I figured Dad wanted engineer and Mom wanted teacher, both honorable professions. Dad would have pressured me into it, but Mom had her dreams, too. Normally quiet about decisions, she spoke up this time. They compromised on Cincinnati.

I packed too much. I told Mom I'd do it on my own, so I ignored her suggestions, smart me. In my pocket, a large nickel-plated medallion, raised four-leaf clover on one side and Pittsburgh Centennial 1916 stamped on the other. My lucky charm… couldn't go without that! Dad got it at the Centennial celebration as a teenager and he'd treasured it. Giving it to me meant a lot. As I began to board the Silhouette, he handed it to me and solemnly shook my hand.

"Thanks, Dad!"

"Take care, son." Uncharacteristically, he hugged me. Mom had tears and a hug. They waited until I cleared the deck, waved and turned to go.

Cincinnati; I'd never been there. Goodbye, Pittsburgh! I'm heading for a clean city, no steel-driving smoke, no grit that got on clothes and up nostrils and in eyes and no matter how hard I scrubbed it seemed to get into bed with me each night.

On deck, I looked the big steamship over. The straight-grained teak deck shone with a deep luster. All the rest of Silhouette spoke of its new, racy design, a steamboat made of Pittsburgh steel. Fastest upriver steamer, the glowing brochure said. Three-day run to Cincinnati. Expensive. Small cabins, but comfortable and well-appointed. Two big boilers below, a side-wheeler. A hundred and forty feet long, beam twenty-five feet, narrow paddles. I had to find a way to get a gander at those boilers, see how they connected to the drives. Maybe...

Dad knew the ship's captain. They met socially and since Dad never did anything without a reason, I bet he'd furnished the steel for this behemoth. I determined to learn all about this wonder of the age and impress him with my knowledge on our return.

I took the envelope out of my pocket and looked at it again. Captain Theodosius Platzenfager, it said. I knew the message. It read, "Teddy, This is my son, Carl. Put him to work if you can find something for him to do." He signed it, "Phillip." Just like Dad, didn't like any Renquist sitting on his laurels. Privately, I liked the idea just fine.

Sailors stopped me a couple of times as I made my way to the bridge, but when they saw the captain's name on my letter, they let me pass. The captain turned out to be on the smallish side, a bit heavy in the middle, but he had lively eyes and that walrus mustache in vogue. He appeared very German. He reminded me of the little old winemaker newspaper ads I'd seen, but I sensed steel in his demeanor. He took the letter I handed him, read it quickly and addressing the letter, gave out a belly laugh.

"Ja, Phillip!" Yup, German all right, and the kind of man Dad would like instinctively, a man in control.

He looked me over and then said, "I haf something you can do. Here." He reached into an alcove and handed me a ship's manual.

"Es ist das boot under you. Es ist our maiden voyage. Try to discover something wrong with it." Again, he laughed and then turned to answer a question from the helmsman.

Over his shoulder, he said to me, "Take das buch to your cabin. I shouldn't have need of it." I thanked the captain and went immediately to Cabin Two on the high deck below the bridge and started turning pages. I read charts and diagrams, all the captions and much text. I absorbed quickly and soon couldn't wait to compare theory with reality.

Ships had always fascinated me and on my own, I'd spent much time studying hull and engine design. My math is excellent and I had little trouble with the conceptual diagrams and graphs.

The ship's horn sounded. Fifteen minutes. I studied for another twelve, put the manual down and went to the rail to watch us get underway.

With a final blast, the two funnels belched black smoke. With a jerk, the big paddle below me began to move inside its massive hood. Up and over, up and over, hypnotically. Each paddle made its trip around the hub, grabbed more water and rose again.

Turning away, I took a chance. Going directly to the bridge I got the captain's attention and told him I'd like to see the inner workings. I explained my desire to compare what I had learned in the ship's manual. His raised eyebrows, not in disbelief, but in friendly challenge, and said he would quiz me.

"Kommen."

I followed the captain to the overlook forward. Rapid questions, length, width, engine size, capacity, speed, fail-safes, crew and passenger complement, location of lifeboats, pump extinguishers. I only failed the specifics of emergency disembarking. The manual didn't cover it.

"Ja, gut," Captain Platzenfager said. "Come, let us stroll."

We walked the deck. I took note of the stanchions and pipes, bulkheads and the step-up, sealed wooden doors with the thick porthole windows. We went into the heart of the ship, saw the boilers, inspected clanking, rotating mechanisms for power transfer, skirted men working hard shoveling coal into the fiery maw of white-hot furnaces, others reading gauges and making minute adjustments. In the end, I could see how a plan first put to paper translated into a physical wonder like Silhouette and I came one step closer to becoming an engineer.

Near midnight, two days into the Cincy run, the starboard paddle caught a large submerged log.

The force imparted by the paddle threw the log at the hull and breached it, tearing the metal skin at its weakest point between its ribs.

Water poured into the engine room and it flooded in minutes. The pumps couldn't hold and soon the swirling river began to sink us. Afraid of explosion, the captain signaled "Abandon Ship!"

The nightmare had begun. We'd traversed a remote stretch of the wide river. I saw no lights on either side and each shore only a different shade of black with the nearly gone quarter moon, they seemed miles away. I'm not much of a swimmer. The crew launched the lifeboats and set the passengers out onto the river, yelling for them to get away as fast as possible. That left fifteen aboard, the crew and me.

To my dismay the flaw the captain challenged me to find came to me. Like the Titanic in 1912, there weren't enough lifeboats or life preservers. I would have to swim for it.

I shucked my clothes down to pants and tee shirt and dove in. The shock put my nerves on end. I hand over handed it, hoping I headed for the nearest shore, hoping I wasn't swimming around in circles, hoping I'd see a lifeboat somewhere. I neither saw nor heard one.

After a while my arms got tired and I tried shouting, but no one came. Close to exhaustion, I gulped muddy river water and spat it out. I thought; I'm not going to make it. Mom…Dad… A different kind of darkness descended.

The glint from an empty wine glass I saw first, and then the familiar comfort of my living room. I shook my head, trying to rid my brain of the awful dream. As I stood to go into the kitchen, something jingled in my pocket. I reached in pulled it out.

Bemused, I stared at a large nickel-plated lucky charm with a raised four-leaf clover on one side and Pittsburgh Centennial 1916 stamped on the other.

"Oh, my God! How...?"

Buttermilk Junction

Calvin Hobbs walked out of the inner room of his store, past his counter and the empty cracker barrel next to it. He opened the front door and looked out, glanced at his chickens and sniffed the air. Smelled like snow.

He'd just finished stocking his shelves. He had enough stock to keep him solvent and as he had the only gas pump in the region as a magnet for business he knew he wouldn't likely go out of business.

Like most years since the crash, 1937 had been a struggle. 1929 started it with that Stock Market debacle, but it really began in 1933. All told, thirty percent of the working population lost their jobs. That amounted to almost fifteen million breadwinners. His face crinkled as he thought of it and he got a touch of acid stomach.

The crash affected everybody in the country. Those who worked hand to mouth in the east and west suffered right away as the lords of industry curtailed their losses and tried to shore up their dwindling fortunes. It took a while for the Great Depression to get to Hoosier country, but it got there. Hoosiers weren't a wealthy lot then or after but they were brought up with good values and lived them.

Calvin suffered his lot stoically, the shortages, the hobos passing through, drifters and grifters, some looking for a day's wage, some looking for trouble, some looking to take what little he had. His wife passed in 1935. Being young when he married, his four daughters had long since moved away east with husbands of their own and left Maude and him to run the store. He didn't hear much from them these days, but he knew their husbands were gainfully employed.

Not funny how the best and the worst in people came out in bad times. It severely tested the hard-working locals he knew. He kept a rifle over the doorway behind the counter for the visual but found it much easier and faster to draw his pistol from under the counter on the few times danger threatened. He'd had to wave it a few times to convince a few his store wasn't a charity, but he also knew desperate people took desperate chances, so he'd gotten used to sleeping lightly.

The drab fall scene met his eye, everything dirt brown, the trees shorn of their leaves, waiting silently for winter. Soon he would stop leaving his door open during the day for his customers. He glanced at his "Open" sign on the nail to the left of the door and then turned to the right to read the mercury thermometer on the wall. The days had been mild up to now, but he'd had to build a fire in the pot-belly stove the last few nights to ward off the chill.

He heard a faint chugging sound and Marty Coombs "26" Buick sedan came into view, raising dust. Looked like their weekly pinochle game would be on time.

Charlie Smith's buckboard wagon sat tied up at the rail. He'd arrived fifteen minutes before from the next farm over. He sat at the careworn table in back shuffling his friend's deck of cards. He seemed to enjoy shuffling. Kept his hands busy. His horses would be fine for a time.

Calvin briefly observed his Ford Coupe sitting beyond the pump. He'd filled the car earlier to make a run to Mavis Peavy's place a couple of miles south. She had gout and since her husband died seven months ago, he would drop by to make sure she was okay. He'd bring her a few groceries and they'd pass pleasantries. He fancied her a bit and thought for a few seconds about how lonely it had been since Eleanor died.

The speck grew and Marty arrived in a cloud of dust. He parked and got out.

"Cooling off," Calvin called.

"Fortnight from November," Marty yelled back. He sniffed the air as Calvin had a couple of minutes before. "Snow coming and not far away."

"That's what I'm thinking." Calvin did an awful lot of that thinking stuff.

Marty stomped up the steps, careful of the broken bottom one, edged his way past Calvin and joined Charlie at the table.

He called back, "You gonna fix that step?"

"Presently." They were, all three getting on in years and the step, over time, became a standing joke. "Ain't killed nobody yet."

He heard the guffaw from inside and the edges of his mouth crinkled.

Calvin tarried a few moments while he dispelled the range of his thoughts. He thought about where he sat in life. Indiana didn't thrill him, home or no home. Folks hereabouts needed gas to get around and the next closest working pumps were twenty miles north in French Lick. Every time he thought he might retire, he decided, nope, he'd stay open. Gotta do something.

He'd thought about selling, but nobody wanted a ramshackle property in one of the poorest counties in the State. He went in, closed the door and lit the kerosene lamp above the table. "Almanac says we're in for it. Predicting early snow and lots of it."

"Read that." Charlie said.

"Speaking of reading..." Calvin let the sentence dangle. The men looked up at him.

"Herb Stower came by yesterday afternoon

with the mail and dropped off a recent copy of the Indianapolis Star." With no electricity or paved roads, regular news didn't get into the county often.

"And…?" Marty said.

He pointed to the counter. "I read this article on what's going on in Europe and I'm bothered. That fellow Hitler's causing a lot of trouble over there and that Roosevelt fella says he won't get America involved. We're supposed to keep out of it, but you read what that reporter says and it sounds like that Hitler fella wants an empire all of his own."

Charlie piped up. "And you're thinking they won't keep it over there."

"That's what I'm thinking."

"So what about the Neutrality Acts Congress passed?" Marty asked.

"Sounds good on paper, but it's only paper."

"Don't this country have enough problems?" Charlie said.

"In spades!" Marty said, and slammed his fist on the table.

Calvin went on. "And what about Japan. Looks like that crowd's trying to conquer the entire Pacific Ocean and everybody in it."

Charlie said, "I don't follow. They're on the other side of the world. That'll never touch us."

"I'm trying to think about my kids and their husbands. We may be about done, but they've got a future." He paused and then added, "I hope they do."

The other two thought for a moment and nodded. That part didn't sound good at all.

"Not wishing, but it would take a lot of pressure off at home. I imagine men would flock to the Army training centers if the lid blows off just to have something to do."

"I suppose, long as you're okay sending our boys off to fight and die. Better be worth it." Marty said. "Look, can we play pinochle now?"

Calvin sat down at the table while Charlie's busy hands continued unconsciously to shuffle the cards. He said, "I sure hope Congress doesn't outlaw this game like it did during the Great War."

Charlie looked over at Calvin.

"Did they?"

"Yup. Germany. That's where pinochle came from."

His game partners stared at him.

"Well, damn, then. So deal!"

No Joy and No Justice

"Justice! You don't think I should have justice?" I ask.

"It's not a question of justice," my wife replies.

"Is that how you see it?"

"How else?"

"Look, let me tell it again for you. I think you may have missed something. I left the house at seven-thirty, right?"

"I was sleeping. I wouldn't know."

"Indulge me." I might have sounded a little exasperated right about then. Fact is; getting stopped by the police on my way to work for no earthly good reason had misplaced my sense of humor.

"It was beautiful out. I left the house and proceeded down Milton Road, as always." I stressed the word.

"Yes?"

"I'm getting to my point. You digress all over when you're talking and I listen, don't I? Can't I at least give you the background first?"

"First, I question how much you listen. Second, I don't digress. I get to the point. Third, you got stopped and the policeman gave you a ticket. What else?"

"You are so cold," I say.

"I'm not cold. I have to go to the bathroom and you're holding me up."

"What's that supposed to mean, you don't want to listen to my reasoning?"

"Not really. I'd rather go to the bathroom and then go downstairs and sew."

"You go. I'm not going to say another word until you get back," I say. "I'll be standing by the cellar stairs to make sure you don't slip past me."

"Really!" My wife grimaces and gives me that look she has perfected over our years of marriage. She heads down the hall. My mind is in turmoil, thinking about how best to explain it to her.

In a couple of minutes, she's back. I block her at the head of the stairs and gently take her by the hand. I lead her back to the kitchen, pull out a chair and seat her. She looks at me suspiciously.

Once seated, she says, "Okay, if you must, get on with it."

With a grandiose gesture, I begin. "I left the house early. Plenty of time to get to work. I'm only going 45 at the time, slower than anyone goes on this road, except in a snowstorm."

"Yes?" my wife can barely contain herself.

"Right. So I get to the big hill and at the bottom, by Duck Pond Road there's the Statie. He flags me down. 'How fast were you going?' he says.

That's after he asks for my license and registration. I'm suddenly thinking what a lousy day this is and how does this cop have the nerve to stop me here. This is my road, doesn't he know that?"

My wife gives me a humorless smile and says, "Go on."

"Well, I tell him I'm not watching the speedometer, I'm watching the road like a good citizen should. I tell him I'd just come down a big hill and maybe I went over the limit a little but so what, I'm going slower than anyone else I know.

"The cop is serious, like from another world serious. I hate that, people with no sense of humor. Reminds me of you sometimes."

"Don't go there!"

"Yeah, sorry. Okay, so he goes around to the back of my car and writes down the license plate number. Who did he think I was, a mass murderer or something? I look at my watch. Oh, man! Gonna be late! My boss is gonna be pissed. Since I can't believe this cop was ever happy in his life, nobody's happy. I'm thinking he went straight from an abusive family into the Police Academy."

"Please! Some people are serious about life, you know."

"Not me! Not enough time for that."

"You mentioned justice…"

"Yeah. So the creep gives me a ticket for going

ten miles over the limit. I tell him again what I said before and I ask him, doesn't this represent entrapment or something, deliberately hiding beyond the edge of a hill to catch some driver who never hurt anybody and was just trying to get to work, which, by the way I would be late for now.

"The cop gives with the stony stare like he's daring me to say another word. I reassess my position relative to law enforcement. I ask him if he's through with me and can I get to work?

He says, 'You can go.'"

Silence.

"Well, I leave, going real slow, kinda like flipping my tail at the guy until I get around the next curve and he can't see me. Then I pile it on. I'm going sixty as I head down that long hill before Beach Street."

I pause, deciding. "Uh, this is what I didn't tell you."

"What?"

"I got stopped again."

"You're an idiot."

"Thank you. I already know that. My point is; this is definitely entrapment. The Staties have this rigged. Isn't this double jeopardy or something?"

"Generally, going up against the law isn't smart. Were you speeding?"

"Well, maybe."

"Then you deserve what you got."

"Great, two tickets in one day and my wife sides with the law. There ain't no justice here or anywhere!"

"Did you expect sympathy?" She looks at me. I look back. We're finished here.

Earthquake

I'm just back from the States on business. I'm a day early and it's 4:30 in the afternoon but I'm anxious to get back and see what's going on in my practice. I glance at December on my desk calendar. All okay. I tear it off and see January and I smile at the circled date, Wednesday, January 13, 2010.

My secretary circled it. I prefer circling the day I leave. I know she misses me. She knows I appreciate being able to look at the previous month first for loose ends. Just in case.

Today's the 12th and Fanny isn't due in the office but she's already taking care of me. Accumulated mail lay neatly on my desk, three rubber-banded stacks, magazines, unimportant and important mail.

My Fanny; so organized.

I sit in my leather swivel chair, pick up the third stack. I leaf through it. Ah…

Placing the stack aside and with delicious anticipation, I thumb open the letter in my hand. It's addressed to Francis duPreaux, Attorney at Law, 1151 Main, Port- au-Prince, Haiti.

I carefully remove the letter and a check for

$40,000. I look at the check for a moment and smile and then read the letter. I feather touch the check with my lips. This paycheck will help my ailing checking account. I drop the envelope in the wastebasket.

The check and confirmation letter means I can keep up the payments on my villa in the hills. It means no change in my life style. I'd been antsy about that. I think anyone thinks lawyers don't live hand to mouth sometimes, they are wrong.

I open the large windows in my office to let in the beautiful day. Clean air wafts in gently. Bird sounds drift in with it.

I'm taking it slow, but suddenly I sit stock-still. Wait. Something's not right, no sound, no movement. The thin letter in my hand is forgotten. The trees? No. The birds have become quiet. It feels like hushed breath. 4:52 p.m. Why did I look at the wall clock?

I let the paper droop in my hand. My attention drifts to the window.

My two transplanted trees, looking almost odd in my nearly treeless country flutter softly. I see two sparrows sitting amongst the leaves, their heads cocked to one side. They are listening. What are they hearing?

My brain goes searching, trying to grasp it. Then I feel it and my eye immediately goes to the half-full glass of water I'd put near the edge of my desk. Did it move? Yes. A little circular pucker appears and it moves from center to outside edge in the restricted space like a raindrop eddies out as it strikes the calm surface of a pond.

I connect with the stillness. I watch the glass. The water smooths out, but now I'm agitated. My first day of school as a child comes back to me, a day when my queasy gut told me I was scared of being thrust into this new thing called school. Mum-ma had told me it's okay to be scared and I'd get over it, but I never forgot how it felt. This is different, but it carries the same gut sick feeling.

My gaze goes back out the window; the birds have flown. My eyes return to the glass. Smooth. No, the little puddle moves again. Tremor? They happen. Look where we all live on this island on the edge of a deep ocean trench. Yet, this time I get a flutter of fear?

The birds know. They have sensitivity. My eyes go to the finished ceiling and I think about my three-story building right in the heart of Port au Prince. It's not quakeproof. I knew it when I bought it, but the price overrode any other caution.

I think I should leave. I push my chair back and start for the door.

Then, big, massive, wrenching, sudden, huge motion! My feet come from under me.

Now sprawled on the floor, my mind reviews a short article I'd seen months before. We were ripe, it said, and it's going to happen any time now. What did that mean? Get scared? Leave the island? How does one leave their country and their livelihood? I filed it away, dismissed it, but now I could see every word on the page again.

My office becomes dusty as things begin to detach. A rolling motion, like a wave appears in the floor and my carpeting buckles and the wave passes under me, throwing my body several inches into the air. The desk jumps, my leather swivel chair upends and my file cabinets empty. All this I see in an instant.

Bathed in adrenaline, I yank myself to my feet and dive for the open window, thanking my lucky stars I decided on first-floor offices four years ago when I bought this building.

Not that I didn't know. I didn't believe. How do you forget about business as usual when no one knows when the big quake will occur? How do you figure it? Answer: you don't. You live each day like it'll never happen and until it does, that's what you do.

I go out headfirst and roll as I hit the ground. Pain, left shoulder. I ignore it. I visualize tons of cement fragmenting above my head, plummeting toward me, trying to bury me before I can get away. The thought gives me wings.

I gain my feet and sprint across the street toward the middle of the little grassy park I glance at and appreciate every day. Now cement blocks rain around me. A small fragment hits me on the head and my mind starts to go black, but I have momentum. My body is on autopilot, terror-stricken, beyond thought.

Three stories of mass, cement and glass, furniture, rented offices, my place, my livelihood, my history, my success, destroyed in seconds. No time for tears. I have to preserve my life. I have to survive. Sobbing from effort a hundred feet away, I fall to the ground. In a moment or two I twist enough to watch my building settle into rubble. A dust cloud billows toward me.

From the corner of my eye I see other people streaking into my safe haven. My head hurts and I feel blood running past my right ear. Words on a case file come to me, something about toxic dust. Oh God! I rip my shirt open, pull my undershirt up over my nose and shout to anyone around me to do the same thing. Everyone's in shock. A couple of people do what I did, but most are stupefied, arms slack, disoriented.

My hearing expands as I come back to myself. Now I hear crashes and screams. So many dead, so many dying. I have lost my building, but I have saved my life. I look at Port-au-Prince, my city in rubble.

I bury my head in my hands. Now I can cry.

My Old Farmall

Pa had got real tired of plowing the fields in the south forty with the horse team. Kept breaking the plow on New England rock 'cause the horses would keep pulling afore Pa could say "Whoa!"

Them horses got mired often enough to hold up production and Pa with a mighty yank, his big farming muscles bulging, would have to cuss them out of the mire with a "Gee!' and a "Haw!" Then he'd lose half a day heatin' up the old forge so's he could fix the blade. Happened time in, time out.

So Pa bought a Farmall tractor, brand new. He got a good price from Jed Wright, who owned the West Torrington Sales Company. Hezekiah Brown, a friend who had a big farm up in Goshen told him that the F-14 tractor Jed showed him that day was a tip-top fine machine.

"Never mind tryin' to convince me, Jed," he told him, "Hezekiah says it's good, it's good. I'll take it."

Pa and me, we jawed about it days when we worked the fields together after I got my size and some muscle on me. Pa said Jed couldn't shut up once he got started telling a story, so Pa listened and I got to hear about it mor'n once.

Story goes, Harvester started selling them in Texas in '24. They were good, Jed said, so it didn't take long before they sold 'em East of the Mississippi and then up in our neck of the woods. Pa bought a bright red one, but said they was gray before. He said Harvester figured red would catch the eye and I'm thinking it did, right enough.

Once he got the tractor, it didn't take long for Pa to see how quick he could stop when he caught a rock and his time spent at the old forge went down a-mighty. He told us mor'n once old Molly and Dolly didn't mind retiring.

Pa spent about thirty years clearing all the rock out of that big field. He'd tell us them rocks would rise up out of the good earth every spring like the Devil's own children. He knew the frost be heaving, but he'd go on about how Providence must be agin him. Over the supper table Ma and us kids would listen to him cuss the day he started that field.

But Ma knew him and let him rant, "Does him good," she told us kids quiet like, 'cause Pa didn't have much humor to him come end of day.

"Everybody's got to let off steam," she said. "Your Pa works hard."

"How come you're nice, Ma? How come you don't get mad like Pa?" we asked.

She'd laugh and say, "I have my moments."

Sweet lady, steady as they go. She made sure Pa attended church regular with her every Sunday. Said he needed a bit of the Lord's blessing toward the end of the week. Said all that cussin' wasn't good for his soul.

After Pa put the horses to pasture, he'd hook up the small wagon to the back of the Farmall, throw on a couple hay bales for seats and drive us down to the Methodist Church. That church sat pretty as a picture in the hollow at the bottom of our hill, its big old steeple risin' tall down where the roads crossed.

"Reaching for God," Ma said.

Ma and Pa made going to church like a summer picnic. That kind of made up for our fire and brimstone preacher, Reverend Teasley. That man went on for three hours every Sunday before it seemed he'd run out of his own steam.

The war came and Pa got deferred as the only breadwinner in the family. He did his war duty by givin' over a part of his crop.

He'd say, "For the boys overseas." He wanted to go fight for his country. It bothered he had to be home. I saw him longing now and then.

Ma had a different tack on the subject. She didn't say much, but we knew she raised her eyes from time to time and gave thanks that she could keep her man home.

That Farmall tractor kept a-plugging and every so often Pa would lay a hand up against the red paint and give it a pat like he used to with Molly and Dolly. Then he'd stare off, remembering how it used to be.

Every Sunday the Farmall pulled us to church. Ma sat on the wagon with us five kids and never complained—even when we were older and knew she suffered from the miseries. She'd just keep a smile and watch Pa up there, sittin' proud atop that tractor's metal bucket seat, working that big, flat wheel. She'd just quietly change position to ease herself some when we hit a bump.

Pa loved that woman. He set no store by another and when she got sickly after we'd all finished our schooling, he did his best to ease around the bumps on the rutty dirt road down to the village.

Time came when Pa couldn't work the fields anymore and with Ma bedridden with the cancer that finally took her to Heaven, Pa'd sit by her bedside one, two hours at a time and just hold her hand.

'Fore I forget, I'm Clay. Me, the girls, Abigail and Mary and my younger brothers Charles and David made up the Malcolm Smith family. As first boy, I stayed to run the farm. It was the way of it then, and since the others had to make their own way, they spread away like oil slick on a pond.

About then the war in Vietnam broke out and both my brothers enlisted in the Army. I recall the president called it a "police action." Never figured it, except people say things to make them sound like not much. We got a letter from time to time, but the official one came one winter's day two years after they left home.

Both killed in the TET Offensive; couldn't get out of Saigon in time. Letter said they were heroes, saved half a platoon, awarded medals. Of course they would. They were Pa's boys. He never had any truck with cowards.

Ma passed the month before that awful letter came, a blessing that she didn't have to find out about her boys. Pa had little to say after that. He kind of sunk into himself. Right after Ma had gone to her reward, he seemed to give up. He stopped being hungry. I couldn't get him to eat and I let Abigail and Maude know, but they couldn't get him to go on either. We knew he wanted Ma. One night he went to sleep and didn't wake up. We buried him in the family plot next to his woman, our family of seven now down to three.

The girls married local and made it a point to bring their families to celebrate Christmas at the old farm each year. After our parents passed on, they continued the tradition and they were good company, as I never married. I kept the farm going and it did well. Truth is; the farm and me was all the partners I ever wanted. I bought a bigger tractor with more power and thought about retiring the old Farmall, but it meant too much and I couldn't do it.

Now we're twenty years into the new century

and me and the Farmall are both of us past eighty. I'll swear that old red beast is in better shape than I am. I just finished spiffin' her up and that Farmall red looks like new. Shortly I'll truck her over to the Goshen Fair.

Entered her in the tractor pull. She'll do fine. She'll make me proud, just like she did for Pa.

From John, with Love

Agnes Livermoor broke down again. Tears fell on her silk sheets. She would not leave her bed today.

Oh, John, she thought, *why did you leave me? It's so hard since you left.*

That day she began the long road down. Now she lived in a lightless world of melancholy, barely perceiving her three remaining servants. They rattled around the gradually deteriorating estate, glimmers nearly matching the ghost Agnes had become.

Like a tape with no end, she recycled the events of her darkest day, her brain excavating the past horror every day for the next four years. Sitting propped on her silk pillows, her damaged mind replayed it again.

It began on October 24th, 1929. The New York Stock Market took a plunge. The very wealthy bought up stocks to stabilize it, and the market rallied, but confidence seesawed. America lived in a financial bubble, its roots dug deep in American soil from coast to coast, but bubbles have little substance and in the end they can only burst. The downward trend continued. Five days later the Market collapsed.

John Livermoor, Agnes' brilliant, up and coming financier husband with offices on Wall Street had been the source of many a news story in the New York Times and associated news sheets. He'd made millions. He had an amazing following. He could do no wrong.

So, had he missed the signs or simply ignored them?

The London Stock Exchange crashed the month before. More than three thousand miles away, he didn't believe it would touch him. Or did he?

Brilliance aside and as human as the next man, he compelled himself to excel at what he did. Within the financial crucible there existed a life separate from most men. Insulated, yes, and he, like most of the favored few fed into the coming train wreck thinking they could somehow avoid or neutralize their part in it.

The morning of the crash he sensed it. He knew it was about to come down around him. That morning John made his final deals, not with his cohorts on the buy and sell floor, but with his lawyers. Before the market opened, he called Kenneth Growville, his most trusted attorney, and added a codicil to his will. It had to do with money he'd squirreled away in secret places only he knew to access.

Many men who held the power of the purse kept separate records. He made Ken party to his secrets and on his lawyer's solemn vow – and ten percent of the proceeds – he filed the right papers in places that would assure his wife's continued life-style and protect his estate.

Two days after the crash John made his last headline. He walked past his Secretary mumbling, "Be right back."

A trip to the bathroom? It barely touched her consciousness. He returned moments later, entered and closed the door to his office.

After a few silent minutes she heard a shot. She rushed in sudden fear into his well-appointed office. Slumped over his desk, she saw blood pumping from John's head and watched his desk surface turn crimson.

The horror of it passed through her shock and she screamed. After that, confusion, police and hours of questioning, the shaken and saddened woman was released to go home.

She donned her coat and left the building. As she took her coat off at home she discovered a fat envelope in the pocket of her coat. On the face of the envelope John had written. "Open immediately in private."

She followed his directive. There were several envelopes inside, the top one written to her. It explained his reason for suicide. He left her a check reflecting that her services would end, but he wanted her compensated for the wonderful job she had done over the years. It was a very large check. Cash it immediately, he said. He instructed her to get the other envelopes to the people whose names were on each, lawyers, friends and finally Agnes, "From John, with Love."

And now, sitting in bed four years later, Agnes recalled every word. John explained his actions and what he had done to protect her from the wolves he'd contended with in the world of high finance. He told her he'd made many enemies, that it couldn't be otherwise amongst driven men, and that his sacrifice would turn them away from all he loved, his wonderful Agnes and the estate he had built. He had no other choice.

'You are strong,' he'd said. 'You will go on to a better life."

Agnes's world shattered. She retrieved the note she kept in her night stand. She knew him now, after death. He'd done it all for her, for their lives together. She held it for the reality it offered. She didn't need to read the tear-stained missive again.

His dogged pursuit of financial wealth did it. He'd seen the signs like other smart insiders, but he couldn't rise beyond the depth of his compulsion. One more deal and he could sit back and enjoy; there was time. But you see, after one more deal there was one more deal, and then another...

She hadn't been that strong, after all. Her high-powered husband, light of her life, steady provider, lover and benefactor through their twenty-six years of marriage made her a showcase and the envy of those around her. But being a wonderful hostess wasn't enough. She'd only excelled in that capacity because of John and his business needs.

John had made a single mistake.

"Oh John," she moaned, "I would have let all this go, moved to another country and lived in a hut just to have you. Didn't you know that?" She'd thought it many times and uttered it before, but the innocence in her only came out vocally after John died.

People shook their heads when they passed the mansion where she lived alone. What a death! Suicide is ugly for the taken but survives forever in the living.

She withdrew. She consumed food only to exist. Otherwise she lived consumed by sadness. She had nothing of value left. She wanted to die.

The bell chimed downstairs. She couldn't recall when it had rung last. She heard muffled conversation. Soft steps made their way up the long winding stairway. A pause. Then a knock on her bedroom door.

"Ma'am, there is a man here to see you." the maids voice.

"I will see no one," Agnes replied through the door.

"Begging pardon, Ma'am, I think you should.

The man was quite insistent."

Who could he be? "Have him identify himself."

"Ma'am, the man said he had come to return a favor and when you saw him you would know. He entreated me to give only that message."

"I don't understand."

"Ma'am, please see this man. May I enter?"

"Very well..." The door cracked open and the maid came to her bed. Her face sagged to see the remnant Agnes had become, but then brightened.

"This man is special, Ma'am. Let me assist you into a dressing gown. Allow me to seat the man and let me tell him you will see him. Please, Ma'am."

Such forwardness from her meek maid created a spark of interest in Agnes. She'd had no thoughts besides the dark ones she lived with for so long, forever, she thought, and for just a moment she felt challenged to rise above her melancholy.

Who could he be? From somewhere deep inside, she felt a desire to know. She shoved aside the bedcovers, planted her unclad feet on the Persian rug at her bed and stood.

"Assist me to my bath chamber and say I will see him in the Drawing Room."

"As you wish, Ma'am."

Sparked by a curious energy she'd thought gone forever, she took time to straighten her hair and apply blush. Putting a light shawl over her dressing gown, she made her way down the winding staircase.

At the doorway she peered in and immediately recognized the newly installed President of the United States sitting casually, apparently enjoying the opulent room's paintings. She watched him knock the ashes off his cigar into a nearby ashtray. Her heart did a little flip.

Hearing a soft sound at the Drawing Room entrance the man turned, saw Agnes and said, "Mrs. Livermoor, I presume."

"Mr. President."

The maid assisted her to a seat and left on Agnes' nod to prepare tea.

"Mrs. Livermoor, I'll get right to the point. Your husband earmarked a significant sum of money for use in my campaign should the winds of fate point me in the direction of the presidency. Mr. Hoover has not pulled the nation back from the brink and my advisors have told me we hit rock bottom a few weeks ago. They told me they needed a strong man with new ideas and chose me. My family backed me, of course, but John's initial injection of cash made a huge difference in my getting the nomination. Before the tragedy, I had earmarked John for a Cabinet post. Subsequently caught up in politics, I lost track of his widow.

"I did not know of your situation until very recently, when a retired attorney by name of Kenneth

Growville contacted me. We met in private and I became aware that you had not moved on as John believed you would. I came to entreat you to come to Washington and visit with Eleanor and me. You will like her. Specifically, I wish to honor your husband in a declaration before Congress and I desire your attendance."

"Mr. President, your appearance has overwhelmed me. I must have time to think."

"Of course, dear lady. And please, call me Franklin."

The maid entered silently with tea, set places on the low table, poured and departed.

They sat and sipped quietly for five minutes while the shock of the meeting wore off. Agnes' private thoughts burgeoned. How often had I been the centerpiece of John's parties? I remember Franklin as an ambitious younger man getting started in politics. He didn't stand out, but I recall him as energetic and hopeful and now look at him.

Roosevelt was content to let the silence lengthen. Agnes Livermoor would be a big assist to his future simply as a reminder to so many who had owed John so much. And, he thought, it will help scrub the past clean for John's method of demise and give me an edge with four Senators whose votes I want in the upcoming session. This New Deal I'm working on has to pass. Too many out of work.

Agnes had no thoughts of subterfuge in the

moment, but newly animated, she saw a possible end to her misery. She would do it.

"Franklin," she started, "I would like to make Eleanor's acquaintance, and getting away for a time I expect will improve my mood. How soon do you wish me to leave?"

"The next session starts in two weeks. Can you be available then?"

"I believe so. Thank you for coming. You have brightened my day."

Roosevelt left after an hour of chat. The three remaining servants watched from a respectful distance, and on their faces were fixed and hopeful smiles.

What Anger Hath Wrought

I drove angry and distracted, too fast for the road.

On a twisting curve my SUV's wheels left the pavement and the large rock I hit sent me careening off the road. I jammed on the brakes and stopped. The car tilted at a steep angle, rocking gently on some part of the undercarriage. It stopped.

Panic faded and reason returned as I realized we'd come to rest. I pulled the emergency brake hard, put it in Park and turned off the key. Then I sat.

In my side mirror I could see rusty, rocky terrain. Ahead of me, nothing! I carefully tried to open my door. Jammed! Sounds intruded and my mind flashed to the back seat where I'd tethered my two children in their government-approved car seats. Their screams of fright made sparks in my brain.

I turned slowly. I felt a shuddering vibration under me. I stopped moving. It stopped. My heart pounded in my ears. My wits went to work at light speed. I couldn't climb into the passenger's seat. Too dangerous! I would have to get into the back. Balance: the most important word in the world now. Over it all I listened for the grating sound that would signal my car begin to slip into the chasm.

"Kids!" I shouted above the sounds. "Kids, lean back in your seats. Daddy wants you to lean back."

Two-year-old Jakey and five-year-old Gracie were beyond reasoning. They yanked back and forth in their restraints. I felt small tremors shudder through the car. Then I saw Gracie's hand move to the seat disconnect.

"No," I shouted. "Gracie, don't move. Don't move at all."

Her eyes were wild and I didn't know if she heard me. My fear escalated. She would come away from the seat and reaching desperately, she'd try and come into my arms and it might send us into freefall.

Her hand stopped.

Anger at my wife's infidelity caused this; my driving too fast, my foot tied directly to the hate boiling in my mind. How could I drive like that with my children in the car? I'm not rational.

Betrayal isn't nice; it ripped me up, but to be reckless with my kids…that's stupid beyond belief. I gulped air and got a grip.

In a more reasonable tone I said, "Kids, Daddy is going to crawl over the seat to you. Sit still, please. Here I come."

Jakey looked at me for the first time and through his tears he put his arms out. Gracie, already a natural mother at five, turned to look at her baby brother and her arms went to comfort him.

Good, Gracie's finally processing.

I leaned slowly toward the back seat, shifting my weight onto the balls of my feet and twisting my body, trying to move back by inches the rocky fulcrum on which the car rested. I tried to cross one leg over the other. It stuck. Working it past the ankle hurt and pain rocketed up my leg. I froze until it abated. The shoe took off a little skin.

Don't sweat the small stuff, I thought.

A little shudder and another grating sound. I froze. The car moved a couple of inches. My heart leapt back into my throat. I balanced; immobile in a position so awkward my leg began to cramp. My eyes clouded and I bit my lip. Oh damn! I gingerly laid my body through the seat separation, ignoring my children who shrieked with fear at the same moment. Bump, shudder, stop. Sweat now poured onto my forehead and my hands began to feel sticky.

The driver's side damage meant I couldn't try to get out that side but the passenger's side appeared intact. Halfway over, I recalled that I had the child locks engaged. I couldn't open either door from the inside, but committed, I had to finish my climb. I'm not a big guy. Even so, with the kids in their car seats, I had little room to work.

"Gracie, honey, Daddy had an accident and I need you to do something for me. Can you be a big girl and do something I ask you to do. You're Daddy's big girl, right?"

She wiped a sleeve across her nose and her little hands touched my face, feather light. She nodded. So fragile in this instant, and our lives depended on her. I hoped she couldn't know that.

"Gracie, you can release your seat now. Go ahead."

She looked at me with her little mouth open and her tear-streaked face tore at my heart, but she did as I asked.

"Now, honey, I want you to do something I've told you not to do before, but this is an emergency. You understand emergency, Gracie?"

She nodded and I tried a smile I hoped she would believe.

"Daddy, I'm scared."

"I know, honey, but you have to do something for Daddy now and if you do it we'll be all right."

"Okay, Daddy."

"Good girl. Now what you have to do is go over and open the door on your side."

"In front?"

"Yes. You'll be okay. Daddy has to stay here to balance the car."

"Why?"

"Because we're tilted and Daddy will help keep the back end down by being here."

"But won't it tilt if I go up in the front seat?"

"No, you're little and it won't tilt if you go."

"I'm scared. Can't you come with me?"

"No, honey, I need to be here. Do this for Daddy so we can get out of the car, okay?"

Gracie started to cry. "Daddy, I can't."

"Sure you can, honey. Remember how you swung from the bars at the playground during the summer and you were so high up?"

"Yes."

"You were so brave. You can do this, too." I tried to keep exasperation out of my voice. How much time did we have left?

Gracie shivered a little and then climbed into the front passenger's seat.

"What do I do, Daddy?"

"Honey, you need to get out of the car on your side and go to the back door. It will open for you, but first reach over and turn the key like you've seen Daddy do before, but not as far as starting, okay?"

She reached for the key and turned it. The radio came on, some local country station. Wang-a-dang-dang guitar sounds filled the car. Gracie jumped, sat still and then looked back at me, eyes wide, fear palpable on her little face.

"You can leave that on, baby. Now reach over to the switches on the door and put one finger on each one at a time, but don't press anything until I tell you, okay?"

She was getting into it and I saw her fear begin

to disappear. Doing something constructive helped. Jakey, nearly overcome by my bulk had quieted, for which I was grateful.

"Gracie, the one your finger is on now, push it down." She did. The passenger's window went down.

"Okay, now push the one behind it."

The rear passengers' window went down. I couldn't imagine how she handled the situation in her mind, but my chest swelled with pride. One more exit, just in case.

"Gracie, get out of the car now from your side and come to the back door and open it."

She opened her door. As it started to swing wide something occurred to me. Door hinges are a fulcrum!

I said quickly, urgently, "Gracie, hang onto the door. Don't let it open wide."

Fear in my voice translated to fear in the child. She grabbed for the door and it pulled her outside as it swung. She made a little yelp as her feet touched the ground and I know she stumbled. The door slammed forward hard. The car began to move.

"Gracie!" Anguish tore from my lungs.

The little girl recovered her footing and raced to the back door, which opened easily. The car slid steadily forward. Five feet…four…three, toward the yawning abyss.

I jumped out and turned to gather Jakey in my arms. Oh God, his harness! I reached for it but the moving car pushed me out of the way. I fell on my hands and knees onto the gravel.

My face a stark picture of horror, I watched the rear tire pass by my hands. The car gathered speed and then, in a breathless moment it left the ground and plummeted down…down…down!

I thought I heard a little sound from the car, I couldn't be sure; a fearful screech that sounded like "Daddeeeee!" but Gracie's shriek of pain and loss is the sound I will never forget, so long as I shall live.

The Cookie Jar Incident

This is much later and I'm driving south and my mind is reviewing what happened back then and then BLAM! The right front tire on my 1996 Chevy blew out. I got stopped okay, but bad timing.

I called AAA on my cell. Then I sat.

I'd be late picking up my daughter from her mother for our weekend. Divorce is disruptive and the wrenching aftermath, trying to make a small child believe that daddy living in a different state and getting to see her once a month is normal doesn't cut it. At four she wants to know why daddy can't be around all the time.

Elsie went for the divorce to get her own life back. Not my fault. When the Taliban caught me, I disappeared from all but the memories of my platoon mates. They knew what happened and being Special Ops they couldn't say a thing.

That's the problem with covert operations. "Nobody knows nothing," as they say. Yeah, the officers do, but they let others know what they want them to know.

I got back, part of a few pawns exchanged by a couple of governments for political reasons about which they lied to the public. My life had changed and I couldn't do a thing about it. They debriefed and rehabbed me and sent me home with healed injuries and PTSD. I got help through the VA and eventually recovered as much as anyone does.

Being away for four years eating dust and not having a good time in Afghanistan, I learned from the letters they gave me at the Post's dead letter office that she'd waited for three years. She said life had been tough and she couldn't wait any longer, that she believed I died thousands of miles from home and she still loved me, but for Molly's sake she had to move on.

The divorce followed about the time she wrote her last letter to me, a sorrowful and tear-stained missive. She said she'd met a wonderful man and she planned to marry him. She asked my forgiveness. I did the math and despite what she said, I think she started looking a lot earlier than three years into my silence. Thinking back, I'm glad I found out at the end of my prisoner time. The thin thread of Elsie and the baby kept me going.

I wanted to see my daughter. It became a driving force in my life. The tree had been cut down, but it still had roots. I had a four-year-old child. I went looking and found them. They still lived in New Jersey and I had an apartment in Hartford, Connecticut, only a couple of hours away.

I embarrassed her the day I showed up at her home in Ridgewood about noon. I didn't see the bell right away, so I knocked. She opened the door. I should have called first, I suppose, but my thoughts were messed up and I didn't want to be put off. I'll remember that meeting forever.

It started, "Hi, Elsie."

I thrust my trademark single red rose at her. Her face twisted in total surprise. Emotions flicked across her face, first her astonished look, then a guarded expression and then a hint of fear. She recovered fast.

"Jake, oh my God!"

I could see her thinking fast. She involuntarily looked at her watch. Husband coming home early? What gives? Maybe someone else? I did a bit of research on the new husband before I decided to blast in without notice. The rose? It shouldn't matter? In my heart I had doubts, but it was my trademark and I wanted to be upbeat.

Carl worked for Bank of America in the City. He had a management position. What I knew of BOA convinced me I'd never want to work there, not if I wanted a life. So, why the look I caught? Lonely? Found a diversion? Naughty girl?

I wanted to think of Elsie as I had when we married. Two years into it with her about to deliver our first child, the Afghanistan thing heated up and

I got the call. I knew the blush would be off the rose by now. No telling how she'd had to live until she hooked up with Carl.

My concern heightened, thinking of how Molly fit into the equation. Elsie taking care of her properly? Molly happy? What about Carl's attitude toward a ready-made family? People don't automatically stray. There are reasons.

Behind me on the street a car slowed, stopped for a moment and then sped up and left the area. I caught Elsie's glance and a momentary pained expression before her features straightened out again. She had someone not her husband. My happy expression disappeared. Pretty obvious her "diversion" just left.

"What the hell!"

She jumped into the breach. "Jake, I thought you were dead."

"For all intents and purposes…" I said. I stared at her.

More hesitation and then, "Why are you here?"

"I think the more important question is what's going on with you? You got a lover?"

"Jake, it's not what it seems?"

"The hell it isn't."

She chose that moment to burst out crying. Sobs wracked her body. I resisted holding her. Eventually she got control and settled down. She motioned me in and closed the door. Turning, she led me to the living room, a nicely appointed place with expensive furniture. It reflected in my mind the status of my ex-wife and her BOA-captured husband.

Dissonant notes lay on a floor littered with toys. It showed the stressed side of Elsie and spoke to the life she had accepted in marrying Carl as an apparent go-getter. I could picture Elsie frantically picking up Molly's toys minutes before Carl came home. The dichotomy spoke volumes.

"Where's Molly," I said. I wanted to see my daughter.

"Please, Jake, she's sleeping."

"She's my goddamn daughter, Elsie. I want to see her."

"She won't know you."

"Doesn't matter! I want to see her."

"Could you at least not wake her?"

I nodded. The child hadn't done anything. I wanted to see how she looked, watch her breathe. I wouldn't touch her. She led me to a decked out room of pastel colors, a gently swinging mobile revolving above her small bed. Molly. Beautiful child in sleep. My heart thumped and my eyes clouded. My child. Yeah, Elsie's too, but my child.

I looked at her for it seemed minutes and then left the doorway. Elsie closed the door quietly. We went back to the living room. I sat. My ex-wife made a detour to the kitchen and brought in a large ceramic cookie jar. She set it on the coffee table and removed the lid. Apparently she hadn't forgotten that I love cookies.

I watched Elsie's practiced steps around the toy litter. Then, like she realized I'd interrupted her routine, she got an idea and started picking up. As she bent over, daylight through the picture window highlighted a reddish-purple area on her face near the hair line when her dark brown hair fell away.

When she stood, I said, "Where'd that come from?"

"What?"

"The bruise."

Elsie felt her face and winced. "I ran into a door."

"No you didn't. Who hit you?"

Elsie wilted and it came out. The guy who stopped and sped off abused her. He was connected to some gang nearby. She started to cry again, said she had to put up with his advances because he'd threatened Molly. Her sordid story included being ignored by a husband too tired at night to meet her needs and a few innocent stops at a local bar. I didn't like her for that, but just as she finished the telling, all hell broke loose.

A hard knock at the door. Elsie looking frightened but drawn to it, knowing the one person who would be at her door knew the bell would wake her daughter. She opened it. This slicked down guy pushed his way in.

"Hey, bitch, what we got here? Cheatin' on me?"

"Carlos, please!" No more words followed. She started to tremble.

He looked at me. "Who're you?"

"Ex-husband, back from the war."

"Well, move out, soldier."

"Not likely," I said.

"Maybe this will persuade you." He reached in his pocket and I saw the butt of a gun.

Anticipating some move on his part, I grabbed the cookie jar and threw it at him. It glanced off his forehead and shattered on the wall behind him. Surprised by my violent move, as the Glock 9 cleared his pocket, he back-stepped onto a toy xylophone Elsie missed in her cursory pick up effort. It put him off balance.

I vaulted from my seat on the sofa and attacked. This guy didn't want to mess with Special Ops. I'd had too many episodes of one chance for life. I took him down. He got off one wild shot and then I battered him senseless.

A tow truck appeared behind me and broke my train. AAA fixed my flat. I thanked the guy and gave him a tip.

As I continued on my way I finished my reminiscing. I'm not big on anticlimax, but I do like to finish a story. Elsie called the cops. They came and took the guy away. Seems they wanted him for murder. Happy ending? You decide.

An altered version of the girl I married, I told Elsie I too had moved on and I didn't want to disrupt her marriage, although she better get straight with it.

Privately I viewed her as damaged goods, with cause, and Carl could deal with it.

Otherwise, I saw her as a good mother for Molly. I told Elsie I wanted visitation rights. I got no argument. I got a monkey off her back and maybe she could see her way to making some necessary changes. Evidently she did.

I turned into the driveway to her mini-mansion and shut down the engine. In a few minutes Molly and I would be on our way to my home where I could spoil her all I wanted for two days.

I rang the bell. The door opened and a bright, smiling face peered out.

"Hi Daddy!"

Dr. Fustus and the Story-teller

I'm Fustus, Gerald J. Used to be a doctor, a shrink, they tell me. Could never figure why people have to malign Psychiatry by putting some kind of street handle on it...likely makes 'em feel better. Guess that's the whole idea.

Kind of fuzzy these days. Dad lived to ninety-eight and I'm only seventy-nine. I think. Mother and father had good genes. She died at ninety-six. Gotta be me.

Dad never had the advantages I had, never did what I did, never got where I got. It's all relative. I made my bundle and the good life took its toll, no matter what the naysayers say. Big house, lots of acres, two children.

They never visit me. Did something wrong? Must have. They don't live far away...well, maybe they do, I forget. Can't think where they live, but it'll come to me. Maybe it's me. Must be me. Kids visit their moms and dads, don't they?

Valerie Manor, the place they put me after Maude died. Said I was confused. Said I couldn't be trusted outside on my own. Said I'd done...what...?

Said… I don't know what they said. Used to live in… where?

There's a noise up front. I'm in a big room and it's filled with old gray people in wheelchairs. I look up from mine and this skinny young fella with the big smiles says, "Here's Dick," and then he leaves the room and…what did he do before?

"Good morning, everyone."

That guy is here again. Seen him before? Don't remember for sure. All I know is I don't feel good. I stare at the TV set he just turned off. The people who run this place think I need entertainment, so they sit me here with a bunch of chair- bound losers for now and they'll wheel me somewhere else later.

I don't give a damn. Why don't they just leave me the hell alone? They're always poking and prodding me, saying happy things, putting me in front of some stupid game. Why the hell would I want to play stupid games? Screw the games. Take me back to my room.

The guy is younger than me, better shape, but not all that better, gray hair, plenty of it is what I see from where I sit. Now he's dragging the tray table that passes for a podium here. You'd think a rich place like this would have a regular podium. I used to use a podium.

Where'd that come from?

The guy looks up. I see him survey the crowded room like he's making sure his flock is all here. Flock of sheep. Yeah, that's us. Bah! That's funny but I can't laugh. What's to laugh about? The guy starts talking.

"I'm Dick Benton. I'm your storyteller. Today I have a fun program for you, including some stories and some jokes. You like jokes?"

One woman on my left murmurs, "Yeah," like she's programmed. She's always yapping.

I don't look around. There's just this bunch of zombies sitting near me. I don't care. My bowels are in an uproar and I want to be in my room.

I don't like this guy up front. He's too happy. Others filter into my field of view. Lady to my left's got a stony stare, gray hair, thinning, old lady, bad skin. She's a wasted one. At least she's got a chair to sit in. She doesn't talk any mor'n I do and I don't. One on my right is Ralph. His wheelchair matches mine, so what else is new? He'll be snoring soon enough.

The guy up front has a black case. He opens it and takes out papers and a three-ring-binder.

"Do you like short stories?"

The same large woman with a compulsion pipes up. "Sure."

She's speaking for herself. No one else says anything and if I cared, I'd think they wish they were somewhere else, too.

"I have a few. These are stories I have written in order to get better at writing."

What the hell does he mean by that? My gut

hurts. Bet they won't do anything about it. Got to fall over before somebody notices. I'd be happier in my room. Come to think, I wouldn't be happy anywhere.

My boys, Robbie and Jackie. Where are they? Both over fifty, I think. Yes, that's right. Proud of them. What's that guy saying?

"Recently I wrote a story about a subject we all fear, the threat of nuclear war. I call this one Requiem for America. I'll read it for you."

God damn, this guy thinks he's an author! I've got bowel problems and I don't want to be here. Limbo, that's where I want to be. Damn, I'll have to listen. I'm stuck here and I'm not giving my jailers any satisfaction, not today.

"Requiem for America."

The man starts reading. He has a nice style. Says it like he means it.

"I removed my glasses and as my vision blurred, a bright flash outlined my window. The little window in the cellar led to a sunken window-well outside..."

I can picture it. The story drones on...no, 'drones' is wrong, it moves. I forget my discomfort. With nothing else to do, I start to pay attention to the words. The man weaves a picture of a little town in New Jersey across from 34th Street in Manhattan, same street the Empire State Building's on. Been there. Who hasn't? What's he saying?

"So you could stop the booze, Frank?"

I can relate. I used to like Scotch, single malt, good stuff. They won't let me near the stuff now. Damn them all! I pick up the guy's story line and listen more.

"The Africans had a lot of support in America for some reasons I thought were obvious. I also detected a bit of black pride...

Never had anything against blacks, except, they were too easily led by the nose into confrontations with the white population. We probably deserved it. A piece of my background urges its way up. I spent half my career understanding the dichotomies humans face and I helped people get around them. Race was a big game card. Defusing people, that's what I did. They were lit fuses and I had to put out the wick before they blew on themselves or somebody else. Sometimes it didn't work and they blew anyway and it got messy.

"I went to work and worked the day..."

What happened? Damn, missed something.

"I love you, Marge."

Must have dozed off. I feel my body jerk. I come all the way back.

"America's going to hell, Marge. I just realized I've been responsible for all the crap we've been going through. I'm sorry."

Tears, he says. Then he says the character removed his glasses and as his vision blurred...

That was it?

I missed something important, I think. I look around. The big lady's saying how much she enjoyed the story. Others nod and a couple of other ladies say they liked the story, too.

Guess I just didn't get it. The skinny kid walks back in, wags his head and smiles at the story guy.

I hear, "See you next week."

The guy leaves.

Big, strapping aides come into the big room and start wheeling my sad bunch back to our rooms. Finally I can be alone.

Something bothering. Something about that story...

The Mongollan Rim

Name's Randy Trowder. Back a yar or so me an muh mule, Stubborn, left the spread an headed so'west intuh tuh Painted Desert tuh look fer gold. Been lookin' fer yars. Got nothin' fer muh pains, but yuh cain't find it if'n yuh ain't lookin' so I keeps on lookin' yar after yar telling muhself next yar I'll hit it big. Well, I hit it big.

This heah's muh story. I'm goin' tuh tell it like it happened.

Rollin' hills start forty mile south o' Hollbrook. Rim's a bit futher. Hollbrook's not much a town, but Arizona Territory's not much a place, neither. Yuh git past the town limit an out o' sight and no man tuh be seen fer miles around. Way I likes it! Night afore I left I packed muh prospectin' kit. Early on next mornin' afore tuh sun peeks o'er tuh edge o' tuh world, I take a quick feed, close tuh cabin door so's no coyote's come lookin' fer grub and leave me a mess tuh clean when I'm back.

Goin' tuh the paddock, I slaps Stubborn on the behind. "Wake up, yuh ol' bag o' bones!"

Stubborn makes thet whufflin' sound she does

when I disturb her dreamin'. Makes me smile, bein' pardners and all, sounds so human. Complains like a lady.

Right then tuh sky looks like a big, upside down bowl, bright and gray an' a touch o' blue. A few stars strugglin' tuh stay lit still show off tuh the side. Time tuh mosey. Big Red be up mighty soon.

Been out in tuh mountains fer a big part o' muh life. Always stop fer a minute or two tuh watch Big Red slide over tuh edge. Mighty perty sight. Fellas down at tuh town saloon say it's tuh crack o' dawn, but I never heerd it crack. Comes up gentle fer me. Only sound's Stubborn breathin'an' she don't care.

I ain't holy or nothin', but thet sight's like getting' borned agin, tuh me. Gives me a good feelin'.

I pack up Stubborn and we light out. "Let's git ground afore it heats up out thar, mule," I says. "an don't fret, them stars'll be back t'nite, right enuf."

The creak o' tuh packsaddle and now an' then muh pot rattlin' agin muh pan makes a comfort. Them's sounds I kin live with. Bettr'n people talking'. Twenty yars, more, them sounds comfort ole Randy. They's jest Stubborn an' me. Ain't like I don't cotton tuh people. More like I don't need em', except occasional, like fer grubstakin' an' maybe play a hand o' poker or two, an' yuh know, coupla whiskeys down tuh the Adobe.

Town folks call me Sourdough. Thet's me all

right. Face full o whiskers, clothes full o dust an' I guess I look a sight tuh the locals, but I got whut I need and the desert don't ask me tuh dress up none.

Got tuh let on muh secret. Randy Trowder's getting' rich this time out. Said it afore, but this time's different. Got me a map tuh a gold stake. Won it fair an' square. Full house beats three of a kind and thet's thet. Ever now an' then I pat muh shirt, so's tuh feel thet map under the buttons.

Fust hours cool an' goin's good. Stubborn sashayin' along with her head down thinkin' nothin' I bet. Me, got muh eye on the horizon, looking fer anythin' fer whut I ought pay attention. Figgered we'd make tuh Mongollon Rim country in two days. One thing Stubborn ain't, it's fast, but I take a lot o' stock in my gal. Stays with me all tuh way. Saved my hide mor'n once.

"Picked us a good one, Stubborn."

Tuh mule's ears perk up an' turn back towards me. Her hoofs make a kind of clip-clop I'm not thinkin' about but they's a comfort all the same. Give me a change in gait an' I'm right thar lookin' fer a burr or stone or somethin' botherin' her. Nothin' out here but thet grainy red dirt now, but on tuh mountainside, more likely.

Tuh day gits on, hot, like em' all. Seen so many I pay em' no mind. Desert's big distance, long treks, one foot past 'tother and we gets whar we goin.'

Stubborn and me stop fer a bite around noon.

Pour grain in tuh leather feedbag an' hook up, then I kin grab a chaw o jerky fer me an' a sip o' water. Die quick wi'out it.

Sun heads west an' we're makin' decent time. Evenin' comes an' tuh stars come out and tuh day cools down. Nothin' like them stars on a nighttime desert. Glory be! We keep goin' fur three hours more. Walkin' in starlight's easy. Sky above's blazin'. Some ways it's better'n day.

I sets no fire the fust night. Grain an' water fur the mule and more jerky an' water fer me. I take off Stubborn's pack an' let her be. She got no place tuh wander, sides, we're pardners. Pardners take care o' one another.

Got no worry about animals, not tuh-night. Mountain lions, other pesky varmints up in tuh mountains, not on the flat. Yeah, furry critters an' scorpions, but I don't worry none where I spreads muh blanket. I lay down an' look at the stars fer a few. They shine so bright I think I kin reach out an' touch em'.

Night cools down right handy. Hot day, cold night. I wrap up against tuh chill and think on how I ain't gitten younger. Afore I go tuh sleep, the map spreads out in front and I kin see muh strike. I kin almost smell it. An' I think about thet game in Hollbrook in the spring an' how I left thet cowboy settin'. He couldn't do nuthin'. I had him "aces up," as they say.

Funny thing, I prospected the same area nigh ten years afore an' never found nuthin'. But thet don't mean a thing. Easy tuh miss a crease or outcroppin' prospectin'. Then muh thinkin' turns down and I drift off.

Fust light wakes me up. Me an' Stubborn'll hit the Rim in another day. Two more, mebbe less, an' I'll be rich. Muh mule is fifty feet off with her head down, dozin'. She hears me stirrin' and her ears perk up like they always do.

"C'mon over here, Stubborn, let's eat." The mule looks at me an' don't move. Makes me recall why I named her Stubborn.

"Git over here, yuh mangy varmint." Stubborn gives me a bray and I doubles over laughin'. When I get aholt o' myself, I grab a handful of grain an' put some in muh pocket an' walk on over tuh her. She nuzzles muh hand and goes lookin' fer more. Tuh other handful I sticks in front o' her nose and she follers me back to muh camp. Dumb mule! Works every time.

I throw on her pack an' tie it down and soon enough we're on the trail again. Another hot day, one thing yuh kin figger on. Don't rain mor'n once in a blue moon out here, just big yeller sun an' meltin' heat.

Come nightfall we're in tuh low hills, mesquite country. Plenty o dead stuff lyin' around fer a fire, an' now it's a real good idea, what with big varmints skulkin' around at night. This time we stop before night comes on. I pick up plenty of wood an' strike a Sulphur match tuh some tinder. Afore long got a roarin' fire goin. Goin tuh treat muhself tuh hard tack an' beans tuh-night. Keeps a man goin'.

Now I got tuh stake up Stubborn. Cain't have some mountain cat screamin' and have dumb ole Stubborn light out. Thet mule kin be right skittish. Took two days tuh hunt her down last time.

Yuh know tuh old saying, "Fool me onest, shame on you; fool me twice'st, shame on me," right? Well, old Randy Trowder don't git fooled twice'st.

I feel under my shirt again. Map's such a comfort.

Colder then usual fer a June night an' feels good. Ringin' my circle with mesquite puts me inside my own paddock. Don't expect trouble but no use invitin' it. Lived a lot o years payin' attention. Still n' all, Bessie feels good tucked intuh the blanket with me. Thet old Enfield is a straight shooter. Ole Stubborn'll let me know if somethin' sneaks up durin' the night.

Now, human kind's the worst. Sneak up quiet, blast yuh in yur bedroll an' think nuthin' of it. Old Stubborn like as not wake me up fer man smell. No fear o' thet in these parts. Puma an' coyote's another thing. Big trouble up north, gangs robbin' trains an' killin' people. Nothin' down this way anybody wants, 'ceptin' me.

In tuh mornin' afore tuh sun's up, I look at the stars agin an' wait fer Big Red tuh git muh bearin's. They's a long arroyo heads west along tuh base o' tuh rim. Half a day, with luck, Stubborn an' me'll be in tuh right place to start lookin fer tuh landmarks on tuh map.

"Stubborn, won't be long afore yuh'll have a Mex beat silver collar. How'd thet be?"

The mule looks at me like, "Shore, I understand yuh, pardner. I'd like thet."

Tickles muh funny bone, dumb mule.

We head west. Not long afore tuh goin' starts gittin' rough. Now me an' muh mule'r goin' up an' down an' bein' pushed side tuh side, follerin' no trail at all. In muh head I kin see tuh way an I keep glancin' at tuh sun tuh make sure I don't git turned around. Trail map's only a line on this piece o' hide, but I knew I'd git thar, 'cause I been around these hills aplenty.

We stop fer vittles at high noon. I turn Stubborn out tuh find what she kin in the sparse grass around and I eat cold tacky agin. Gotta be careful tuh keep tuh grain fer places what don't got no feed near. I got a good sight on whar we're goin', so I kin relax a bit an' tuh direction's no thang.

That night I keep Stubborn near me and big Bessy by my side, cocked and ready. I sleep with one eye open, 'cause we be in the hills and thar's real danger now.

Well, two days git along and tuh mule an' me are right under the rim past them foothills. They's a jumble o' rock perty near everywhere now and finding a path tuh walk is takin' a good bit o time. Meantime I'm lookin' fer vein gold in every likely spot. Mebbe I got old eyes, but they sees like a eagle.

I kin see yonder tuh thet fur mountain 'tween two out-juts in tuh rim whar it curves. The rim's tuh muh back. Muh map say I'm in tuh right place. Time tuh start searchin'. I find me a small closed in place with some grass and stake Stubborn tuh a long tether an' off I go. I git my pick an' start circlin', wider an' wider. This ain't whar I been afore.

I climb over rock an' through narrer ways 'tween boulders twice tuh height of a tall hombre. In places it opens out, an' then closes in agin tight. Don't look like gold bearing rock, but yuh cain't tell. I git back tuh Stubborn after eight hours and he's brayin' fer water. Waterskin's half gone. If'n we don't find good water in tuh next couple days, it'll git tuh be a worry. Bin through it afore; we'll git through it agin.

By tuh end o' tuh day I'm bushed. I git some tinder and wood from the near scrub and build me a small fire. It's amazin' how anythin' kin grow in this forsaken country with near no rain a'tall. I gotta scratch muh head wonderin'. An' I hain't seen coyote or mountain track so fer, but they's around. Yuh kin bet on it.

Next day and tuh next I work the rim but I cain't find nothin'. Nothin! Well, Randy Trowder ain't a quitter. No, sir! Muh fortunes out there somewhere. Goin' tuh keep on gittin' 'til the gittin's good. Makes me think I'm stubborn like Stubborn. Thet makes me laugh all over again. I'm thinkin' it's mighty good I kin laugh. Some days it's all I kin do.

Five days now we're in bad country an' nuthin' so far. Thet night we gets a bad scare. Mountain cat sneaks up thinkin' he smells a fine hock of mule and wants a piece.

Stubborn's staked up nights, 'cause I'm a dead man she gits loose. Like I say, me and her', we's pardners, only sometimes I don't think Stubborn knows that.

I'm sleepin' not twenty feet from muh mule. Night chill, no wind, no sound anywhere. Anyways, Stubborn catches Puma smell when the cat's right near tuh jumpin'. Muh mule whirls around and gives out with a big sound, like tuh stand old Randy straight up!

"I'm awake, consarn yuh, Stubborn!"

Then I'm thinkin', Randy, we got trouble. I'm full awake now an I sees this low form comin' fast at muh mule and no dern cat's gonna git a piece o' muh mule and I grabs old Bessie and fires off a round inta tuh night. Stops thet cat sudden like an' it goes up in tuh air two, three feet. Got no time tuh sight fer a second shot so I fires agin' at the movin' cat and prays quick I'm not goin' tuh hit muh mule.

First shot's still ringin' in muh ears when I git the second off. I'm thinkin' it's a near miss, but the bullet creases across top of tuh cat's back an' it screams an' drops right whar it got hit, 'cause sudden-like, them back legs goin' no place. Then it screams agin and I know it's a cat's death scream.

I'm outta muh blanket thuddin' barefoot in the moonlight tuh finish the varmint off, but no need wastin' a bullet, 'cause thet cat dies right afore my eyes.

Now, Stubborn's eyes are wide and she's tryin' tuh loose the tether an' I don't blame her none. I goes up tuh her an' starts talkin' soothin' like an' I git her tuh stop stompin' around, but I know she's still scairt an' I knows she'll stay thet way 'til I drags thet cat carcass off someplace whar he cain't smell it.

When tuh excitement's over I got me some fresh meat an' I'm good tuh stay fer more days. Trouble is; water is the tellin' thing. One more day without water and Stubborn and me'll have to head fer home.

Six days out an' I got nothin'. Dern dratted map! Dern dratted cowboy. Fooled Randy Trowder, gol-dang him. Git muh hands on him an'…oh bother! Shame on me! Right about then I give thet dead land a fine string o' cussin' fit tuh turn muh own ears red. Goin' back empty agin. Dad rat it!

Muh sainted Ma told me if'n I get all riled up

I should take some deep breathin' an' so thet's what I do. After a bit I'm tolerable better. I git serious and go through my pack agin fer the umpteenth time. Water's still tuh problem. How I figgered it'd change by lookin' another time I don't know. Gotta head back.

Got a couple weeks food, low on grain and water fer three days, so I heads fer home out straight, northeast. Tuh rim hangs over me fer a long time but gits lower as I head fer the desert.

Well, four hours inta tuh mornin' I'm climbin' over this jumble of rocks when I stumble an' catch meself about tuh put muh eye out on a sharp rock. I lay breathin' hard for a couple, thankin' muh lucky stars I didn't break somethin'. I'm low tuh the ground an' looking inta a crack an' in tuh crack I sees a glint, like metal. Tuh mornin' sun shines part in and I pick meself up and say to the mule, "Stubborn, you hold up pullin' on me. I hanker tuh look in thar."

Stubborn don't want tuh do nuthin' she don't want tuh, but I git her attention and lead her around tuh whar a big rock is closin' off the hole. Then I tie a rope to the rock and git Stubborn tuh do a little pullin'.

Tuh big rock moves 'nuf fer me tuh see clear-like and I gits inta tuh hole an' lordy, lordy, I knows gold when I sees it an' this here's real gold an' lots of it!

I shouts tuh Stubborn, "Yippee! Thar's gold in them thar hills after all." An' I laugh an' whoop and toss muh hat inta tuh air an' off the surroundin' hills muh voice comes back on me like thunder. Sudden-like I'm thinkin' nothin' like givin' away the location of yer strike. Dumb, Randy, dumber then Stubborn!

I git a mite jumpy 'cause o' tuh dern fool thang I done, so I moves off tuh a place under a overhang whar I think nobody kin see me, but mebbe I kin see them an' sets a spell an' listens good. I keeps the eagle eye out fer varmints o' my kind, but after a hour or so I'm thinking nobody heerd me an' I'm safe wi' muh secret. Then I takes out muh map an' tuh spot the cowboy marked was nowheres near this un'.

I goes back tuh muh strike, chips out a few nuggets wi' muh short handle pick and puts em' in muh pack. Mighty fine seam, mighty rich an' thet's me, Randy Trowder, yes sir! Well, now, I'm bustin' at muh own seams an' I cain't wait tuh git back an' file muh claim. But I gotta be careful like. No desert varmint's as gol-dang dangerous as them two-legged ones.

I git Stubborn to help close up the seam I found and then I heads back an' ever so often I looks back to reconnoiter, see whut the land looks like goin' away an' I marks it on tuh map. Goin' back don't seem like nuthin', but the last day Stubborn an' me are on short rations. Muh mule complains but

I don't. Thet's 'cause I got a thinkin' head, not like Stubborn.

Fust thang when I git back I git me a lawyer. They's a good 'un in Flagstaff, I hears, Herbert J. Finnian by name, an' honest man, tuh preacher at tuh Baptist Church in Hollbrook tells me an' if'n yuh cain't trust no preacher, who kin yuh trust? So thet's tuh lawyer fer me. After stoppin' at Little Creek fer a day or so tuh git Stubborn back tuh her prime, I whacks tuh dust off'n muh clothes an' spiffs up, best I kin.

Off I goes tuh Hollbrook an' gits tuh stage fer Flagstaff. I'm aimin' tuh git tuh last laugh on thems laughed at me. While I was in town yuh kin bet money I steers clear tuh whiskey bottle, though it's a mighty big attraction an' muh mouth fair waters thinkin' o it.

At Flagstaff I files muh claim at tuh assay place fust thang. Then I takes muh paper to tuh lawyer Mr. Herbert J. Finian. I tells him whut I wants and listens good tuh him. He says hire a crew tuh work the mine and protect muh claim. I does whut he says an' I hires a fella tuh watch over it 'til I kin get it goin'.

Well, some time's gone an' tuh money starts tuh come in. I built onta muh cabin an' bought up some land nearby, a few hundred acres. Got me a crick an' a small lake, durin' winter season, anyway. Built a real big barn fer Stubborn but she keeps goin' back tuh her little place alongside. Guess she feels best whar she's used to it.

Muh lawyer says real plain tuh me when I'm up tuh Flagstaff, "Yuh got lucky, Mr. Trowder, but if'n yuh want tuh keep it, yuh better learn readin' an' writin'. Yuh want tuh lose it an' be dirt poor agin, keep talkin' tuh way yuh do," he says. Yuh want tuh be somebody tuh go along wi' yuh money, yuh got tuh eddicate yuhself," is whut he said. Only he says it better.

Thet's muh story. Randy Trowder's a rich man now 'cause I did it tuh right way. I listened tuh muh betters. I found me a schoolmarm willin' tuh take tuh trek in from Hollbrook during harvest season when tuh youngsters git out o' school tuh help wi' tuh hayin' an' such. Violet's her name an' she stays in tuh extra room I built.

Readin' an' writin is real hard fer an' old codger like me, but I'm goin' tuh do it, 'cause Randy Trowder don't give up. I'm goin' tuh git eddicated. Can't be tougher then findin' a gold mine, kin it?

Gordon Tuttle

Long before I actually laid eyes on the man, I sensed that my relationship with Gordon Tuttle wouldn't be a source of joy and comfort to either one of us, especially me. What could I expect? His goons had me tied up with duct tape, one of my two favorite products. I love WD-40, too. That's the other one. I felt I should mention it since I brought it up.

Got to hand it to Gordon's boys, using modern technology to do the job. Imagine trussing somebody up with rope when duct tape is used around every home in America. You know, quick repairs to your car's upholstery, covering the split in your kid's bicycle seat, just about anything.

They had me in a kitchen chair. My kitchen chairs weren't all that sturdy, being twenty-five years old and having gone through the rigors of my four, now grown and gone children. Made of oak, my favorite wood, the old brown high-back style meant they were strong, except at the joint points, which creaked from loose screws and failed glue. I point out that they held me tight just fine.

Charlie and John did a good job of making

me part of the chair, I have to admit. Crooks learn stuff about things most people hear or read about, but seldom take time to really get into. I think it is part of the School of Hard Knocks where they learn all that stuff, you know, how to use rope and duct tape, how to torture people for information or just torture them, if that's their thing.

Charlie sat on a chair smirking at me. Charlie wore an outsized blue work shirt and baggy jeans. His belly protruded over where he might have had a belt, but I couldn't tell. I guessed he liked his beer. A disgustingly fat, but very strong man, he kept his eye on me while John went out for cigarettes. There's a packy a block from my house and they sell 'em there. I know because I buy liquor there. Obviously, they sell cigarettes, too.

I don't smoke anymore. Filthy habit. Stinks up a room and the stale mouth you get from cigarettes only works if your wife also smokes like a chimney. Then you're immune, kind of.

'Course, if you're a drinker and she's a smoker, neither one of you would be able to abide the other, I suppose. Fortunately, my smoking wife died of lung cancer two years ago, kind of why I gave up cigarettes and started drinking. Well, not fortunate she died; only that she doesn't have to watch me become a lush. I do miss her. Strange how when you're all tied up, you have time to think about absurd things.

Charlie's a hulking dummy, Gordon's dog. He

likes to hurt people. Evidently Gordon saw value in that, because I picture Charlie groveling at his feet like a lovesick puppy, that type of guy.

The only contact I had with Gordon so far, a phone call I got two days ago, he told me he'd be showing up to discuss money. As I sit looking at Charlie's smirk, I replay the conversation in my head.

"Money? Who is this?" I say to the unfamiliar voice on the other end.

"Gordon, my man." He sounds black. I know, I shouldn't stereotype, but he does. He has that unmistakable inner-city speech pattern. I search my brain, but I can't make a connection. There has to be one. In my business, you don't get to know all the people you affect, one way or another.

"I don't know a Gordon, do I?"

"You gonna soon."

"What's that supposed to mean?"

"You know Dilatania Jones?"

"Oh, her. Yeah, so what?"

"She married to a friend of mine."

"How'd you get my number?"

"I got ways, man. Look for me." He hung up.

I found it a little unsettling. Dilatania Jones borrowed some money from me. I run this banking business, see. You need money and you can't get it from a regular bank, you can come to me. My rates are high, but you got a need, I can fill it, you know? Call it a substandard client loan fund, something like that. Hey, the banks give out sub-prime mortgages. Pretty much the same thing, isn't it?

Jones didn't tell me what she wanted the money for, but I found out later her husband is into gambling and isn't always successful. Not my problem, but I'd been after her for the weekly payment. You know, nice at first, accommodating—for an additional fee, of course—then not so much.

So this morning about seven a.m., this guy John comes to the door. John is tall and thin and clean cut and he's got blue eyes and he's wearing a dark brown delivery outfit that says UPS. He looks the part. I can't remember getting a delivery so early in the morning before, but they got to start some-time. I'm not expecting something, but I have in the past, so I open the door.

I should have listened to that little nagging voice in my head. "Check this out first," my voice says, but I don't.

My voice is right. John pushes me and I catch my balance on the telephone table near the door and by that time Charlie looms behind him and it's all over but the shouting, you know.

That's where we are now. John comes back and I'm sitting, going nowhere. I can't believe this, he lights up outside and has his smoke before com-ing back in. Gotta love these no smoking programs. Even some of the scum are doing the right thing.

Five minutes later Gordon walks in. He's short

and dapper and I want to laugh because he's wearing a zoot suit. Remember them, high waist, wide legs at the top, tight cuff, pegged trousers, long coat with wide lapels and the wide padded shoulders. Remember the zip-up pants bottoms? This guy's out of the forties, for crying out loud. He's got intense brown eyes, kind of bloodshot near the edges and with a little madness in them. In a couple of minutes I figure I know why he's the boss of this pair. He's a take-charge guy, and for his size, real impressive. He gets right to it.

"My friend Lennie found out his wife borrowed some money. He had to take her in hand. Consider it a bad investment. You write off bad investments?"

"Not often."

"You going to write this one down."

"She signed a contract."

"It's void, get it?"

"Let me outa this chair and we'll talk."

"I talk, you listen."

The upshot of my day is I get to live and we forget Dilatania Jones, Lennie Jones, Gordon Tuttle and his two dogs. We go back and forth for a little, but after he calls Charlie over to administer some grinning persuasion, I decide Gordon is right, after all. He didn't exactly break my legs, but they'll be healing for a time and he may be a dummy, but at pain he's an expert.

Win a little; lose a little, like life. It took me six

hours after they left to get out of the tape job. You'd think he could have left a kitchen knife nearby to help out, but I didn't suggest it with Charlie around.

I figure I'd better relocate. I've been known to make good choices when it counts.

The Last Sundown

Through hooded lids filled with pain, I watched the sun begin to set. From my hospital bed I could see through the window, sometimes hazily, sometimes more clearly but then hazily again as I drifted in and out of a morphine stupor that could no longer control the constant signals my devastated body sent to my deteriorating brain.

As much as it hurt me to look, I couldn't turn away. With my eyes I could try to grasp the thing I felt slipping away. Tonight the sun would set directly between the two mountains framed by that window. I had looked longingly at that scene, that beautiful, cruel scene for the past month. I so wanted to be out there, not here in bed waiting to die.

I wanted to be walking, searching, hunting, a thirty-pound backpack on my strong back, my rifle in hand at the ready and a carefree grin on my face. I wanted to be alone, plying through woods of tall Douglas fir, taking long strides and reveling in it. I wanted to smell the smells and appreciate the wildness of backcountry forests with eyes and nose. I wanted to taste my surroundings, to experience it all as fully as it was possible for a human being to do.

Worse luck! My handsome, vibrant young body had failed me. It seemed like eternity now, but only four months ago to the day; I had been given my death sentence.

"John," Doctor Patel had said, "the tests are back. You have a rare form of cancer. The headaches, the occasional dizziness, the bright spots in front of your eyes are an indication that the cancer has spread to vital parts of your body and especially to your brain. We can treat it, but it's going to be a long road." He didn't tell me that it was incurable; that remission was a possibility, not a probability. I wish he had.

"What is the name of this thing I am suddenly afflicted with, Doctor?" I asked.

"It's called Courley's Syndrome. It usually starts in the liver and may remain undiscovered for years. Most standard testing doesn't show it until it begins to manifest its own symptoms, and many times the initial symptoms are confused with other, lesser maladies that make it hard to diagnose until it is in an advanced stage."

"What do I do?"

"You'll undergo radiation treatments starting immediately. In about two weeks the accumulated damage to healthy tissue will cause your hair to begin to come out. When you get into remission, it will grow back."

"Is it fatal?"

"In more than fifty-percent of the cases, yes." Ninety-five percent is more than fifty, right? He thought not to cause me to give up while any chance remained for recovery, I guess. I didn't ask further. I didn't want to know and the thought of pressing my doctor scared me too much.

"Any alternatives?"

"No. It can only be treated in this fashion. I think we have discovered your cancer in time, but with this disease, there are no guarantees. Are you game to go for the program?"

What could I say? Did I want to die? No. I didn't give it a thought. Four months ago. Evidently it was no good from the start, but who knew? Finally, two weeks ago, another eternity, Dr. Patel gave me the lowdown.

Why me? Hadn't I spent my time growing and learning about forestry? Hadn't I learned the ins and outs of living in the wild? Hadn't I gotten my degree and applied to the Forest Service so I could help this world, preserve its resources, be an advocate for conservation? Hadn't I gotten the position, one of great responsibility? Hadn't I started my new career positively, with joy in my heart and a good program to follow? Hadn't I been doing it seriously, making a difference? What did I do to deserve this?

It seemed so unfair.

I remembered what Dad had said when I was

ten years old and I first told him I wanted to be a forester. "Son, grasp life and pull it to you. It isn't fair and it isn't unfair. It's just life and you can do with it what you will. What you do will be the measure of the man you will become. Be what you feel in your heart you must be. If you became a forester, you would make me proud."

I always remembered his words and his wisdom. I believed them and I lived them. Lot of good they did me now. Dad was out there in the waiting room with Mom, my sister and fifteen-year-old brother following the doctor's advice to let me rest.

Twenty-eight years old! Not a long enough life, I knew, but all the life I'd been given. And now I had to die and I could feel my strength ebbing and there was not a thing I could do about it. So tired. Must be close.

My doctor and the doctor specialists he had called in had mouthed their hopes to me over the months. But when they thought I wasn't looking or couldn't see them, they shook their heads and wished they could do for me the only humane thing left; euthanasia. They knew long before Dr. Patel laid it on me.

During one period of great pain, when the morphine cocktail they'd put together stopped working and the doctor ordered something even stronger, I asked him to give me something that would end it for me. All my defenses down that day, shorn of strength, my courage gone, unable to pretend a moment longer, I pleaded with him.

The law prevented him, he told me, not without compassion. It was a heartless law, a mindless thing created by healthy, pain-free people, people who felt none of my pain, people who only caused more suffering, making agony exquisite and unbearable, making it go on interminably, not because they didn't care, but because they didn't understand.

I finally understood. Life was what I had made of it and what I had done had been good. Life always ends and I should have no regrets.

The sun sank into the cleft of the twin peaks beyond my window. A nurse came in and, startled, saw that I was close, closer than anyone had thought. I knew why. I had found my peace and decided to let go. I would slip away at sundown. As the sun's light went out, my light would go out too. I would leave this earth with the sun's last glimmer into eternal night. I liked that thought.

My family crowded into the hospital room and surrounded the bed. Mom and Sis were crying and Dad had tears, too, and like a man he held them back. My kid brother turned away; couldn't handle it. I knew he was crying, too, because his shoulders shook. Great kid. A lot of heart.

The great orb of sun fused with the mountain. It became a tiny, brilliant spot.

I whispered, "Goodbye," and a moment later my last sundown melded with earth's night.

Throwaway Idea

The bright idea comes into my head one sunny day while lying in my hammock. It had rained for three days, a regular deluge, and I never thought it would let up. I had ponding on my lawns, front and back. Little rivulets on my gentle slopes had become major points of destruction. My lawn now looked like some of those ads you see on TV.

"Does your lawn look like the Grand Canyon? You have a serious condition known as erosion! Our product…blah…blah…blah…"

Well, baby, the gentle hill in the back yard washes off to the west and the front lawn to the south. We got it all, yup, both. So I get to thinking about how many back yards there are in America? It blows my mind. Big number!

You want to know? Yeah! It's 66,569,016. That many! And growing. Can't stop progress.

All my life I wanted to start a company. So I'm in my hammock thinking this way on the first beautiful, seriously spring-like day of the new season. Sunny with a few fair weather clouds in the sky and 80°. Imagine; eighty! That's a temp I normally complain about. Too hot! But, you know, on the first day after a cold spell that had been preceded by a seriously cold, cold spell, which had been preceded by an even colder winter, 80° is really, really good; easy to relate to.

Got your attention?

I guess you're dying to know about my bright idea. Here it is. I'm thinking about how we are at the mercy of the weather and there's nothing we can do about it. Get real! There are all kinds of things we can do about the weather. Sure, conventional wisdom is to get out from under it. Most of the world does that, don't they? I'm talking people here, not animals. They're not thinking, not at our level, anyway.

It's so easy; you've got to laugh! I'm lying here in the hammock and this big smile starts across my face. It begins at the left corner of my mouth and trembles across to the other side and my eyes get wide and I can't believe it, like why has nobody thought of this before? All them eggheads thinking and thinking and never coming up with this like simple idea. I'm thinking probably too simple for them. I hear that eggheads are deep thinkers; so of course, a simple thing would blow right past their noses, right?

I got it figured. Anyway, what sheds rain? Plastic, right? Why not get these huge plastic sheets on a roll—purchased from my company, of course— and when it begins to rain, the strategically placed equipment I put up there at the side or back of your property automatically senses the rain and these big sheets come on over the grass and cover it, see? Then let it rain and who cares!

Well, I'm thinking that'll work for big lawns, but what about if people want trees dotting their lawns? First of all, trees shed rain anyway. Not to worry. The object is not to stop rain altogether, I mean, you don't want your lawns to like, die from malnutrition or something. And trees would break the fall of rain, so to speak. The rain's not pounding down doing damage so you let the trees stay. Then you need less plastic. Saves money.

That's not so good. I'm not going to get rich showing people all they have to do is to fill their lawns full of trees and then they won't even get that erosion thing. Gotta rethink this.

Now, how about this? Two rockets take the sheet of plastic and shoot up and over the trees. Viola! No more erosion. Let's see, rockets make noise. That's a downside. And I wouldn't want to set fire to nearby grass and woods, either. That's not going to work.

Okay, how about if my company sells people on the idea of covering their property with Astro-Turf. Now, there's a smashing idea. Short, green grass, never mow, never worry about erosion, kids play on it, no worry about ticks, and if any part wears out, I can replace sections. Ca-ching, ca-ching! Flower beds, no problem. Trees, I can go around them. See, now why didn't anybody think of that before? Am I smart, or what?

Cost? I can offer budget terms and low monthly financing. Nature lovers - who cares! They'll be the ones with the ruts and dead grass patches. Let me figure this out now. Your average one hundred by one-fifty lot I could cover for only $60,000. A deal, right?

No? Why not? Look at the advantages. Wait, where are you going?

Damn!

I open my eyes. I'm in my hammock. When did it cloud over? The first big drops of rain start filtering through the trees and wake me up.

I bolt for the porch before I'm soaked. Damn dream. Whoever heard of plastic to cover a lawn? And rockets? Ridiculous! And why would I ever think anybody would want to replace their lawns with Astro-Turf? Dumb, throwaway idea!

Must have slept a couple hours. I'm hungry. Where's the sandwich spread?

Hapless Hal

I'm Hal. I'm talkin' from the other side. We don't have much to say over there in the world. Too busy tryin' to make a livin'. I was a scout, over there. Pretty good one until…well, I don't want to get ahead of myself.

Anyway, I get over here at the big Hive in the sky and the Chief, the Big Kahuna Hornet, you know, he says, "Welcome to Hornet Heaven. You got a choice. Wanna tell your story or just fool around up here. Understand you had a bit of trauma got you here. Story might help. You're gonna be here forever. Think it over."

So I think it over and I'm thinkin' there ain't no justice. I mean, like, I'm dead. What'd I do to this guy what squashes me like a bug. What I do to him? I sting him? No. I fly around and mess with his head, just for fun? No. I get a bunch of the boys together and buzz that big sucker? No, not even that.

Maybe somebody over here got some sympathy. I'm thinkin', okay, I'll go for it and I give the nod to the Chief.

Wham! I'm standing on a platform and this hall is filled with brothers and sisters and cousins and they're all waiting for me to say something.

I'm a little nervous, but I gulp and start talkin'.

"How'd I get here? I got squashed by some Bigfoot human."

I hear a few gasps and see a bunch of sympathetic nods.

"Look, I'm outside in the big world, flyin' around doin' my thing, right? Blue sky, beautiful day, see an occasional bee at a distance, like big mother Bumble. I wave, she waves back, goes on with her business jumpin' flowers. Hey, whatever trips your trigger, right?

"So I come to this big building. Mosta the time I can't get inside, doors and all, but this time somebody opens a door and I like, jump on the bandwagon and I'm in before you can say Jackie Robinson or whatever.

"Wow, what a swell place to start a hive. I'm flying around and this place is big, real big inside. Sign in front says Elks Lodge, whatever that is and it's all brick and wood. Swank!

"Like, here I am scoutin' this huge room, lots of hiding places, lots of neat places where my clan could come in and make a dandy hive, you know, make babies, be safe, carry on the race. What's it all for, if we can't do that?

"Well, I dive into this one room in the back and I'm all alone and then I'm not alone 'cause this guy comes into where I'm flying around. He's wearing black pants, white shirt and a funny lookin' vest with some sort of emblem on the front with this big varmint sproutin' antlers on top of his head. Huh!

"The guy looks around and spies the keg. He heads for it, grabs a glass and I watch him draw a cool one. Lip smackin' good, I'd say, but not my brew. I drop down from the ceiling where I'm buzzin' around lookin' for attractive home sites like I said and he sees me.

"The guy eyeballs me and takes a sip, sets the 'cool' down and heads out. Well, now, I'm not botherin' him and he's not botherin' me, but like I said he goes and don't you know, in a minute here comes this Bigfoot human and he's got a metal can in his hand. I don't like the look of the can or the guy who's wielding it. Gives me a bad feeling.

"What I do? I done nothin' to him. Just flyin' around, right?

"So I buzz up near the light fixture where I can see the room and all to get back to my searching. Bad choice! The Bigfoot human spots me and raises the can. Out comes this stuff. Gets all over me. Now I don't feel too good. I fly funny and my pins ain't doin' well. What he hit me with?

Okay, so I'm feelin' sick and does this Bigfoot care. Hell, no! He sprays me again. He keeps it up, sprayin', sprayin'. He's like deadly, no pun intended. My wings feel heavy and before you know it I crash to the floor. Yeowp! Here comes Bigfoot and squash, I'm done for.

Next thing you know, I'm on all six in front of Big Kahuna Hornet and he's like, well, sympathetic, but he's tellin' me like it is, 'You're dead. Get used to it.'

Fine kettle of fish. Sayonara, baby. Momma's little boy hits the skids.

I stop tellin'. Can't think of anything else.

"You done?" the Chief says.

"I guess."

"Feel better?"

"A little."

"Well, take off and have some fun, then."

"Okay, Chief."

I fly off and look for something to do. This is forever. No dangers, no challenges, I dunno. Looks boring to me. Well, maybe I can hook up with some cute thing—like that one over there, the bright yellow one with the nice stripes. Nice lashes, too. Oooo! She's givin' me a few facets. Things are lookin' up.

One more thing. Hey, Bigfoot, I'm not gonna forget you. Don't make any mistakes and end up here. Be warned! And the other guy, rat me out, will you? If I find a way, heh, you just wait. Ain't forgettin' you, either.

Le Café DuMonde

Looking over my shoulder, I quickly entered the Café DuMonde. I knew I'd lost my tail. I searched in the dim light for Gaston. There, over by the fake fireplace he sat, yakking with Michele, the cutie, five-foot-three of gorgeous, delectable womanhood. It figured! Leave the guy alone for two minutes and he's after all that's natural.

I'd been gone an hour, not my fault. But my news couldn't wait. I moved up quickly.

"Gaston!" I whispered loudly. My voice carried enough and he looked up.

"Frank, you're late." His face took on a disgruntled look. Why do the French always have to try laying a guilt trip on us Americans? I couldn't go figure on that one.

"No choice. Got to see you. Now!" I turned my right thumb downward. The news wasn't good and I wanted Michele to leave, too.

Gaston caught on and spanked Michele out of the way. She pursed her lips and made some kind of an "Ooo" sound, only it sounded like "Ouh!"

How do they do that? I pursed my lips but

couldn't make that sound. I smiled inwardly in spite of myself. How silly, I thought, bad business and me trying to pronounce a word the way the French do?

I love to hear the French language spoken. It's very liquid and I don't understand a word of it, let alone try to pronounce it. Made me wonder why "M" sent me into this when we have a French-speaking agent in the department. But, I do what I'm told.

So Michele left and I got close with Gaston. In my brief glance I could see the fat man wore a black silk shirt, maroon trousers, the baggy kind I hate, and a cravat. Did it make him look sexy or something? My stomach churned.

I brought my thoughts up, higher than his had been, anyway. Back to business! We had trouble here and Gaston could stop this from getting out of hand. Still, I stayed dubious.

"Tell me what is the trouble, Frank."

"It's your damn French foreign legion, Gaston. You were supposed to arrange for Marcel and Mikel to be at the drop site and out of sight. They're parading around like they want someone to take pictures of them or something. What gives?"

"Oh, ho, ho, Frank! That is the best cover of all. Who would suspect those two of being under-cover agents?"

I wasn't convinced. "No self-respecting agent would act like that here, Gaston. Our prey is going to fly, I'll bet a dollar."

"An American dollar?" Gaston said with a smirk.

"You know what I mean."

"Yes, Frank. You are young and you do not know my people. They are showing themselves to be tourists in a place where you would expect tourists. They will miss nothing. You do not have to worry, Frank. We will be there to catch the "evildoers," as your President would have said."

Gaston laughed again. His belly jumped around. Obscene, I thought, absolutely obscene! How could Michele even look at this misshapen man? I kept it to myself.

In the position of go-between, I didn't feel I was accomplishing much. Still, Gaston and his group had the nod from "M." What could I do?

"Look, my little friend, in twenty minutes, we will have our answer. Sit with me and have a drink. You are nervous. All will be well; it is my promise."

"No, Gaston, I can't. I have to get back to my post. At least I won't be seen."

Suddenly a dangerous looking gun appeared in Gaston's hand.

"Sit down, Frank."

He said it quietly but I caught his meaning, like crystal. Now what, I thought? I sat.

Michelle came over to our table with some duct tape. No smile on the pretty lady, either.

"Put your hands behind the chair, Frank." He

gestured with his gun. I did what he asked.

Michelle took a long strip of tape and expertly bound my hands, first to each other and then to the chair-back. Staying to the side in case I decided to kick, she bound my feet, one to each chair leg. Agent Frank Farber was going nowhere.

"This is for your own good, Frank. I won't have Michele cover your mouth if you promise not to yell, okay?"

I felt like saying plenty, but I kept it inside. I didn't want my mouth covered. I felt a cold coming on and it would be tough to breathe through mucus-clogged nostrils. "I won't yell."

"Good, Frank, that is good."

How had this friend of the U. S. Government so suddenly turned against us, and why? A lot more going on than I had any idea, and I didn't like it. "M" assured me of this Gaston's friendship and that we could rely on and trust him.

I didn't like him to begin with, but in the Service you don't get a choice of bedfellows. I tried not to be judgmental, but he seemed decidedly less like a friend now. Couple of points for my instinct! Anyway, trussed up like this, I could do nothing.

They'd sat me down at the far end of the table in a little alcove where I wouldn't be visible to anyone walking in the door. In the mid-afternoon, customers were few. I thought Gaston would have Michele lock the door anyway, but he didn't. He did put his gun away. Then he turned and kept his eye on the door.

It came to me. He expected someone. So Marcel and Mikel were a ruse! Why did Gaston keep me here? I'd have been none the wiser watching the drop site. There must be another reason. Guess I'm dangerous. Either that or Gaston wanted me where he could see me, plain and simple.

Twenty minutes ticked away. I slowly tested my bonds. Very tight and well done, but I had a fraction of an inch of play. Maybe I could loosen the tape enough to rip it, if I got the chance. I didn't think Michele used a lot of tape.

I'm small and don't look like much. "M" says I make a perfect agent. Nobody would notice me in a crowd. Maybe so, but I'm wiry and strong, too. I don't let on and like I say, I don't look it. I labored at my bonds.

Three things worked for me at the moment. Michele went back into the kitchen to do something. I didn't know where she could be, but she couldn't see me. Gaston had his eye on the door and gave me no attention. The table covered my slow movements.

I flexed my right leg, tightening up the muscle. I felt something give. Ripping tape makes a sound. I tried to rip it gently. It took a couple of minutes of intense pressure. When it felt about to give, I flexed the left leg and did the same thing.

Meanwhile I had managed to gain an inch on

the tape to my hands. Maybe she wasn't all that expert, after all. Maybe they underestimated me. I kept glancing at the door. More than twenty minutes had passed. I noticed Gaston fidgeting in his chair. Nervous or worried?

The pressure of breaking the bonds quietly tired me out, but I got a new lease on it when I felt a sudden give behind me. I'd disconnected from the chair-back. Another two minutes and I'd be free.

Maybe I made a sound. Gaston suddenly looked back at me, hard, like trying to figure out what he heard. He started to get up and check on his prisoner when a shadow fell across the door. The knob turned slowly. Gaston turned back, a faint smile on his face, his thoughts elsewhere. I breathed a small sigh of relief.

A tall, dark, broad-shouldered man entered the restaurant. Behind him came a gorilla of a guy. He must have been six-six and three-fifty. My heart sank.

The first man said, "Ah, Gaston."

"Monsieur le Grande." Gaston, now totally composed and self-assured, stood and shook the man's hand.

The tall man looked at me briefly and then at the restaurant owner. Gaston shrugged and said, "Earlier business. I will finish it later."

They both looked away. I became a piece of furniture.

"Please." Gaston gestured and then sat back down in his chair. The tall man sat across from him while the big man stood behind him protectively, glancing around every few seconds. Monsieur le Grande put a thin attaché case on the table. I caught a part of Gaston's expression. The Frenchman seemed about to drool.

I renewed pressure on the remaining bonds. Suddenly, with a little jerk, I got free. No one noticed. I tested my legs. Yes, free there, too. I brought my eyes to slits, my vision darting this way and that, looking for anything that would help me. It concerned me that Michele had stayed out of sight.

Gaston had put his .44 Magnum in his right side pocket. When the man moved in his chair, I could see the bulge shift. I might be able to get the gun. I thought about it and a plan hit me. I almost smiled.

Meanwhile, le Grande opened the case and took out a fair-sized package. He carefully unwrapped it and removed a velvet bag with a pull-tie at the top. Then he laid a royal blue velvet mat down and opened the tie, pouring the contents slowly onto the velvet. With a small tinkling sound, marquee, square, round and oval cut diamonds poured out. They were brilliant, all of them in the two and three carat range. I'd have bet they were all in the vvs quality.

I couldn't see well and dared not move for a

better vantage. I guessed there must have been ten million dollars' worth of diamonds in the collection. Why Gaston had turned traitor didn't seem so strange anymore.

The traitor pulled a jeweler's loupe out of a shirt pocket and ran his fingers through the pile. He chose one and studied it, put it down and took another. I watched him do it a few times. Le Grande let Gaston check out the diamonds, but kept a wary eye on him. Finally Gaston looked up.

He said, "Yes, they are beautiful. I will have Michele bring in the money."

He snapped his fingers. Michele came in immediately, carrying another attaché case, larger, black and rectangular. From the way she carried it, it seemed fairly heavy. She glanced at me, but did not stop. Gaston took the case from her.

"Merci, mon chere," he said. Michele stood looking at the brilliant treasure below. Her eyes sparkled and she smiled but said nothing. Gaston grabbed her hand and looked up at her.

I saw my chance. I rose from my chair, picked up the edge of the table and heaved it at the three men. I caught them completely by surprise and off balance. Le Grande and his gorilla fell back. Gaston, being slightly to the side grabbed for anything he could. As he turned, my hand dove into Gaston's pocket and I came up with the .44. In the same smooth motion with my other hand, I pushed

Gaston into the tall man and they both went down.

The gorilla gained his feet and pulled his gun out, even while trying to steady himself. I put one between the big man's eyes. He slumped to the floor, twitched, and lay still. One dead gorilla! The gun had a kick like a mule.

Michele turned to run. I didn't want to kill her, but I couldn't let her escape. I put one in her right leg and she went down screaming. I didn't feel right about ruining such beautiful womanhood, but she'd lost my vote as a friend.

I moved around the table and aimed the .44 at the two men sprawled on the floor. Gaston glared up at me, eyes filled with hate. The other man looked at me curiously, as if he couldn't quite believe what had happened.

"Move and die. I'll make it simple." I found a telephone a step away under a nearby counter. Without taking my eyes from the men on the floor I dialed "M."

"Got an interesting crew here, boss," I said when "M" came on the line. I explained where I was and how I saw my situation. I listened for another ten seconds, said okay and hung up.

"Get comfortable. You won't be here long." I glanced at Michele, a little worried. She lay whimpering, her leg broken and too much blood flowing from the wound. I didn't want her to die. I grabbed a sash cord from a room divider, yanked it down and threw it to her. I knew her leg must hurt like hell, but she took the cord and tied it around her upper leg, twisting it into a tourniquet. She screamed again, but held it and the blood slowed.

The tense situation lasted another ten minutes, when two members of my team came boiling through the doorway, sized up the situation and let me off the hook.

"M" came through the door last. "Nice work, Frank."

"Thanks, sir. I just feel bad about the lady."

"You'll get over it."

A Note From the Author

I introduced several fantasies and dream states in this volume to break up more serious stories of human caring, episodes in the lives of some that don't turn out well. Reality is what happens. Light dreamscapes sometimes morph into nightmares, but life is not and should not be serious all the time. Humor in one sense contains the ability to laugh at oneself. It has saved many who were on the brink and about to fall. If humanity were not imbued with a sense of humor, the world would be a sorry place indeed; although to be fair, it's sorry enough as it presently stands. I hope you have found something, perhaps many things within this volume that you can relate to or see for the first time in a different light.

Volume five is done, Volume six will introduce yet more stories that will capture your imagination, I hope as well as they did mine while I wrote them. As always, whether said or left unsaid, I offer my readers my heartfelt appreciation for joining me in these adventures.

www.ingramcontent.com/pod-product-compliance
Lightning Source LLC
Chambersburg PA
CBHW051252250626
47155CB00009B/3264